MW01136841

Florida
On My Mind

Short Stories by Florida Writers

Written by

East Lake Writers Workshop

Palm Harbor Press

Florida On My Mind

Library of Congress
Control Number 2012901226

ISBN-13: 978-1469929958

ISBN-10: 1469929953

Printed in the United States of America.

Contact East Lake Writers Workshop or the individual authors at
floridamind@gmail.com

Cover art by Maureen Lacey

Introduction

Florida On My Mind is a one-of-a-kind collection of original, distinctive short stories written by members of the East Lake Writers Workshop. When our group decided to publish examples of our work under one cover, we selected Florida as a common theme to link the stories. We hope you enjoy reading them as much as we enjoyed creating them.

The Writers Workshop was founded in 2004 and led since then by Deanna J. Bennett, a successful writer and entertainer. Twice monthly, writers meet at East Lake Community Library to exchange ideas and hone their craft. The Workshop serves as a sounding board and a critique group to encourage its members to realize their full creative potential. All writers are welcome. Participants include women and men, young and not so young, beginners and published writers. Though diverse in many ways, we all share a passion for writing.

The Writers Workshop could not exist without the encouragement and support provided by the East Lake Community Library, Palm Harbor, Florida, which provides a meeting place for the group. The writers thank the library management and staff, and especially library volunteer Deanna Bennett whose imagination, encouragement, and hard work over the years have motivated so many aspiring writers to become successful authors. And finally, the writers wish to thank Ruth Duncan who served as editor-in-chief, putting professional polish on our work.

East Lake Writers Workshop

Palm Harbor, Florida

March 2012

TABLE OF CONTENTS

MY FLORIDA VALENTINE

by

Dorothy Ann Searing

I ran down the steps of the City Hall and headed for the beach to take the long way home. This morning's town council meeting was the most contentious ever and I needed to breathe some of that healing salt air.

It was an exquisite mid-February day, the height of the tourist season on the west coast of Florida, and pale-faced snowbirds from the frozen north were everywhere. They hung out in groups wading in the shallow water and lounged about on bright-colored canvas chairs with matching umbrellas.

I slipped off my sandals to wade into the ankle-deep water when a grey haired man, trousers rolled up to mid-calf, said. "Hey lady, you're moving too fast. Got to slow down and enjoy your vacation."

"I'm not on vacation."

Feeling immediate remorse for my rudeness, I apologized to the inquisitive tourist and asked if he was visiting from Canada.

"Yes," he replied. "Did my winter pallor give me away again?"

"That, and your accent," I chided.

He laughed and asked, "And, where are you from?"

"I live right here on the beach, year-round."

"Really? In one of those grand high rises or a huge mansion?"

"Neither. An old forties bungalow!"

"I didn't think there were any of those left."

"Well mine was still standing earlier this morning. And I'm in a big rush to get back there now, so take care, and enjoy your vacation on the beach."

I walked on, looking out to sea. Over the years I'd become quite proficient at politely preserving the solitude of my walks, a handy skill on winter beaches.

The beach right here, so close to town, always maintained a manic, carnival atmosphere during the "season." Tourists ate, drank and roasted themselves in the sun. Vendors, carrying heavy ice chests, hawked ice cream and beer for double the price in the grocery store. And in the sky above, gangs of gluttonous seagulls circled and stalked, ready to steal anything edible they could from the unsuspecting tourists.

"Hey, wait up, Fran!" a familiar voice called. It was Lydia Collins. She ran to catch up with me and splashed everyone in the process. "Oh, Fran, dear, it's so good to see you," she gasped, breathless. Lydia used to live in the old bungalow next to mine but sold it about a year ago, right after her husband passed away. She eyed me up and down from my wet toes to my straw sunhat, and sighed, "You're more worn and tired than ever. It's high time you sell that old place before it kills you."

"Lydia, please! No real estate talk. I just left the town council meeting and it was awful. Besides, I haven't yet recovered from seeing your cottage being hauled away in pieces. I'm all alone out there on Finger Key now."

"Well, of course you're alone, Fran. Everyone else had the good sense to sell. You know, Carson Development is paying top dollar for the old shacks on the beach." Her facial expression said "I told you so" as she shook her finger at me. "They're paying a hell of a lot more than the trash is worth!"

"I prefer to think of my home as 'old Florida' not trash," I answered defensively.

"Listen, Fran, the plan is to build high rise condos on Finger Key and you're in the way. Now that's not such a good place to be!"

"Well, I'm not ready to sell. And I don't think I could bear to watch my beach house demolished."

"So don't watch. Just take the money and run."

"Lydia, don't you miss the old place?"

"No I do not. Any more than I miss the old goat who left it to me. They were both worthless. But I got a good price for that 'itty bitty patch' of sand that it sat on. True beach frontage is rare, you know."

"So you're happy in a condo?"

"Hell yes! I'm in that new high rise way down on the beach, just at the end of Crystal Road. That builder guy, you know the one on the town council with the bushy eyebrows, set me up with a good deal. And I'm not sweeping sand out of my kitchen ten times a day anymore."

I squinted and looked south toward the curve of the shoreline where the huge concrete and steel high rises stood like giant linebackers, ready to block the sea breeze from reaching inland.

Lydia had always been a good neighbor but we were never what you would call "friends." So I was surprised when she put her arm around me and whispered like a trusted confidante, "I just gotta tell you, Fran. People are saying that you act like a crazy woman, cursing and fighting with everyone. Why there's even some wicked gossip about you living out there on the beach all alone with a young surfer."

"What?"

"Yes!" she answered. "Come to my place on Sunday for brunch. You can see my condo and we'll talk. And dress up a bit, dear."

"Thanks, Lydia, but I don't think I can make it Sunday."

"Oh come on. You need to get out more." She placed her cheek against mine, kissed the air and ran out of the water with her shell jewelry rattling, leaving a heavy floral scent in her wake.

I had to admit that Lydia looked great in her bright orange shorts with that tight flowered tee shirt. It seemed that all the ladies on the beach were "fashionistas" now, wearing colorful outfits from a new boutique on the boardwalk. Not me. I felt tacky in old-faded jeans, my hair carelessly stuffed under an ancient sunhat. I heard my stomach growl and, when I walked out of the water up onto the beach, the dry sand sticking to my wet feet reminded me of fish fillets coated with breadcrumbs.

I walked past the empty sand lots where the "spring break" motels used to be. And, further up the beach, the old Shrimp Shack Eatery, that used to host those nightly clambakes and bonfires, was closed and boarded up.

The roar of a jackhammer blasted from the town parking lot so I stopped to join some beach groupies to watch a town worker drill holes in the asphalt pavement.

"What's going on?" I shouted.

An old man yelled over the rumble, "We used to park our cars here all night and make out in the dunes. I never thought I'd live to see parking meters here!"

Not sure he could hear me, I said, "I guess even necking on the beach is a source of revenue for the town these days."

"Yup, you got that right!" he grumbled.

I felt sad seeing how much the beach had changed over the last few years.

When I finally reached the row of new, three-story "McMansions" built on twelve foot high stilts with break-away walls, I plopped down in the sand to rest. Sure, these new homes had that special Key West charm, and they conformed to all the new building codes, but I thought they were still a bit "much" for life on the beach.

I had to force myself to get back up and walk the rest of the way out onto Finger Key. The beach was really quiet out here and the sand was the consistency of confectionary sugar. At the half-way point, I saw my old beach house languishing in the afternoon sun against a backdrop of blue sky and white clouds. When I got closer, I saw the damaged roof and the wood-rot, like giant warts on an otherwise lovely face. And one side of the back porch sagged so much that it actually touched the sand.

This old beach house had always been my refuge. And now it provided a soft place to fall for my young windsurfer, my golden beach boy.

My Tommy was out there now, gliding over the water just beyond the point. He stood tall on the board, holding tight to the frame as he manipulated the blue and white sail to capture the wind. He pitted all the strength in his young body against the forces of nature as his long sun-streaked hair blew wildly in the wind.

It felt great to see him so happy. So great, in fact, that even the rancor from the town council meeting just disappeared. To be honest, I was annoyed even before the meeting started. I hated having to walk all that way into town but my presence had been requested. And after rushing, the meeting started late, the coffee bordered on rancid and the donuts were stale.

The first speaker, a sickly man who looked like he never even went to the beach, read a long list of zoning restrictions, finishing with, "All property owners who violate these restrictions will be fined and charged interest. If the fines are not paid within sixty days, a lien will be placed on the property."

"How neighborly!" I thought to myself.

Then "Bushy Eyebrows," Lydia's friend, enumerated even more offenses that all applied to my old house. Apparently, even the wind chimes on my back porch were in violation of the new noise restrictions. He ended by using my house as an example of an eyesore, a disgrace to the community. "I'm just surprised that old 'cracker shack' out there on Finger Key wasn't blown away that summer when we had those four hurricanes. I'm talking about major safety issues out there."

I told the council that my grandparents built the beach house in 1940 and it had withstood some really bad storms.

"Well Ma'am, that's all the more reason for you to get out now while you can still get something for the old place. Sooner or later, we'll get a direct hurricane hit and you'll be blown to bits."

"I'm not ready to sell just yet," I said. I couldn't sell while my Tommy, my only grandson, still needed the comfort of the surf and the salt air.

"Listen, Ma'am," a well-dressed man sitting right next to me spoke, his breath as rancid as the coffee, "if you can't afford to fix up that old shack, then you had better sell. Do it now and you'll make enough money to buy yourself a little condo somewhere. And we can even make these fines go away. If you don't, the town will attach liens to the land and, in the end, you'll be left with nothing."

I understood now. Someone wanted my land. When I looked around, I noticed that some of the spectators appeared to be uncomfortable. To their credit, they didn't like the intimidation tactics either.

I spoke up again, even louder this time. "Who are you, you arrogant sons of bitches, to want to crush my home and my memories into the sand?"

"It's called growth!" Bushy eyebrows shouted from the council table.

"Well too much growth -- the kind that destroys everything in its path -- is called cancer," I shouted back.

There was no verbal response, but all four council members squirmed, stiffened and moved closer to one another. I'm sure they were afraid that I might do something crazy, maybe even dangerous. Everyone in town still talked about that incident a few years ago when I shot an intruder who tried to break into my house. I only grazed his leg but the weekly newspaper had a field day - portraying me as "a loner, packing a Derringer."

"What is this beach going to be like with just high rises and three story monstrosities with grandiose stairways leading into the sand - and elevators? Like an elevator belongs on the beach! I'm just glad my old house is free and clear so that I can't be forced to buy insurance. That would surely bankrupt me."

"You're a damn fool if you don't carry insurance," another councilman said.

I couldn't afford insurance. I didn't even know if I'd be able to pay the taxes this year. Even with all the repairs that Tommy had done, my old "cracker cottage" might just fall down – with or without a major storm.

I was so lost in my own thoughts about the meeting that I didn't even notice Tommy standing right in front of me, holding the windsurfer over his head with the top of the sail facing down toward the sand.

"Hey, Granna, Mom's here. She's inside waiting for us." Barefoot and shirtless, wearing jeans cut off at the knees, Tommy looked like a clone of his grandfather. I fell in love with Tommy's grandfather right here on Finger Point. He was one of the first windsurfers on the beach, a beautiful golden beach boy. I watched as Tommy detached the sail from the surfboard with care and, almost reverently, placed them both against the back of the house.

We went inside the house where my daughter, Olivia, sat at the kitchen table waiting for us. She looked up at Tommy and her eyes filled with tears. "Tommy, you look wonderful, so healthy and strong."

He kissed her on the cheek, standing back so as not to get her wet. They talked for a while and then he excused himself. He returned about ten minutes later wearing khaki pants, a light blue tee shirt and loafers, holding a small shopping bag in his hand.

"Happy Valentine's Day, Granna." Tommy took a small, red, heart-shaped box of chocolates from the bag and gave it to me. Then he gave Olivia a slightly larger box of chocolates and whispered, "I love you Mom."

Olivia hugged her son and winked at me over his shoulder. And I do believe that she gloated just a bit because her box of chocolates was bigger than mine.

"I'm going out for a while. I made plans," Tommy announced, avoiding our eyes.

As he passed by me, he whispered, "Don't hold dinner, okay?"

I knew that Olivia was disappointed.

When Tommy closed the front door behind him, Olivia and I ran into the living room. We watched through the salt stained windows, like voyeurs, as Tommy met a beautiful young girl in front of the house. Her long, black hair glowed like precious onyx in the Florida sun. They kissed and Tommy gave her a tiny, red, heart-shaped box.

She opened it immediately.

"Oh my!" Olivia said. "Tommy gave that girl a gold heart-shaped locket."

"I paid him for the work that he did on the house, so he had some money. And now, you see, my dear daughter, there is absolutely no significance to the size of the box."

Tommy and his dark-haired beauty walked away hand-in-hand.

"I can't bear it," Olivia said. "I've lost so much time with him and now I'm not even first in his heart any more."

I tried to comfort my daughter. "Oh my dear, don't you know that he will have many loves in his life, perhaps even more than one wife. But he only has one mother and that special place in his heart will always be yours and yours alone."

"You're right, Mom. And if you hadn't been here for Tommy, I don't know what would have happened. You saved his life."

"It was the rhythm of the sea that soothed his tortured soul. I'm just sorry that he had to be apart from you for so long."

"He had to get away from everything: the house, his friends, school, even me."

"He's very different from that angry boy who came to live with me."

"I can see that. His father's drunken scenes and the newspaper stories -- all those lies -- they took a terrible toll on Tommy's young soul. I didn't think he would ever trust again."

I gave Olivia a folder from the coffee table. "I've tried home schooling. He goes to the high school in town for testing."

My battle-worn daughter was impressed. "Mom, this is great."

I didn't tell her how many times Tommy stormed out of the beach house during those first turbulent months or how often I walked the beach at night, searching for him, fearing that we would never see him again.

I said, as gently as I could, "Tommy felt powerless and that made him angry. And just as all youngsters do, Tommy found a way to blame himself."

"I couldn't get through to him the way you did, Mom."

"How could you when you were both in such pain? I made him work off his anger. But it was when I got your Dad's windsurfer down from the attic that Tommy came back to life."

We talked more while I prepared a dinner of fresh scallops and pasta. And while we ate at the table on the back porch, I broke the news about the beach house. "When Tommy goes back home to live with you again, I think that I'm going to have to sell the beach house."

"I guessed as much. But maybe you shouldn't be out here alone anymore."

"Yes, it probably is time to move on. I just hate to cave under the scare tactics of Carson Development. But they'll pay through the nose for this little patch of sand."

"To you, Mom, the toughest old broad on the beach!" Olivia toasted me with her glass of iced tea.

We talked and talked as the sun became a huge red ball of fire, hanging low in the sky before us, allowing a brief moment to worship its power and beauty. And then with surprising speed, it just dropped beyond the horizon, leaving only streaks of color behind. Soon the sky, the beach and the Gulf of Mexico were nothing but deep black darkness.

I lit two small votive candles and gave Olivia a sweater. We stayed out on the back porch to enjoy the sea breeze.

About an hour after sunset, the old front door creaked.

Olivia yelled, "Tommy, come on out back. We're on the porch."

We could hear Tommy's heavy footsteps as he ran through the house. When he appeared at the back door, I noticed for the first time, that he had to duck, ever so slightly, to get under the door frame. Someone was with him – a well-dressed, older man.

Tommy made introductions in his casual, seventeen-year-old style. "This is my Granna, Fran. And this is my Mom, Olivia. Meet, Mr. Carson, Kara's father. You haven't met her yet, but you will. Kara's my girlfriend."

I offered our unexpected guest iced tea but he declined, as he sat down at the table beside me. Tommy balanced himself on the porch railing.

Mr. Carson smiled and said, "You have the perfect spot here with the blackness of the Gulf at night but you can still see lights along the shore to the south."

"Yes, I've always loved that about the view from Finger Key," Olivia agreed.

"Your boy, Tom here, joined our family for dinner to celebrate Valentine's Day. And today is also my wife's and my wedding anniversary."

"Mine too!" I exclaimed. "My late husband and I were married on Valentine's Day right here on the beach. Of course, that was a very long time ago."

"Yes, Tommy told me. He talked a lot about you and your family."

Tommy interrupted to explain. "I wanted Kara and her family to know us. She and I met windsurfing. She's probably the best windsurfer in the State."

"Well, I'd say that you're both excellent windsurfers." Mr. Carson appeared to be adept at diplomacy.

"Are you spending the winter season here on the beach, Mr. Carson?" Olivia inquired, anxious to know more about the family of the young beauty who had evidently stolen her son's heart.

"Please, call me Mike. My wife, my daughter and I just moved here from California and now we live here on the beach year round, in one of those three story monstrosities with the grandiose stairways that lead down to the sand, with an elevator."

I recognized my own angry words from this morning's meeting and felt my face get red hot. But then it all came together. "Mike Carson. From Carson Development?"

"Yes, Fran, I came here to apologize for the actions of my associates. I never authorized anyone to threaten you. And I delegated far too much responsibility. Things got way out of hand and too many landmarks were destroyed. I'm going to be a lot more 'hands on' in the future."

Without looking at his face I replied. "So, you think an apology is enough for threatening me and for destroying a small culture?"

"It was never my intention to destroy anything. My goal was to build beautiful homes in a beautiful place. Things and people got out of hand and, now, I want to fix what I can. Take this house of yours, it's like a forties movie set. It could be the base for a landmark bed and breakfast or it could be moved to the boardwalk. Will you just consider talking to me about how to make things better?"

There was an awkward silence.

"I'll talk to you. But that's all."

"Fair enough. I just want a chance." Mike Carson stood up. "Please, all of you, come to brunch at my home on Sunday?"

"We'd love to come on Sunday." Olivia jumped in before I had a chance to refuse.

"Great. We'll expect you around noon. Don't get up, I can find my way." Mike Carson descended the two rickety steps from the porch onto the sand. But then he stopped and looked at me. "And, just for the record, Fran, I'd also have shot that intruder if he broke into my home."

Olivia, Tommy and I watched the glow from Mike Carson's flashlight get smaller and smaller until it was so far away that it looked like the glow from a cigarette.

Finally, Olivia spoke. "He seems to be sincere."

"He is," Tommy said. "I can see things about people now and I can pick out the truth from the lies."

"I believe you can," Olivia answered.

Tommy switched on the porch light and spread a brochure out on the table in front of us. "Granna, look at this brochure. I took it from the restaurant tonight. It shows the layouts of the condos that Carson Development built down south on the beach."

They were quite nice.

Olivia gushed over the brochure. "They come with granite countertops and stainless steel appliances – no extra cost."

Tommy winked at me. "Hey, Granna, these here are some real nice lookin' cracker shacks."

Evidently my grandson knew a lot more about what was happening on this beach than I thought.

Tommy sat next to me and put his arm around me. "Granna, I'll help you move if you decide to move. But if you want to stay, I'll live here with you and fix up the house. I promise."

Tommy was so like his grandfather that I had to fight back tears. But my grandson was ready to go back home now and I couldn't hold him here.

A powerful shiver racked my body.

"Are you cold, Granna?"

"No, I'm not cold, Tommy. But I am tired. I'm going to bed now."

I didn't sleep at all that night. By morning, I'd made the decision to sell the beach house. I even had a plan for negotiating the best price. Beyond that, well, I wasn't sure! Next Valentine's Day, I might be living in a brand new high rise here on this beach or I might be walking on some exotic, far-away island.

I loved my old house and I was grateful for the life that I'd lived here. When I looked out at the Gulf, I could still see Olivia, as a little girl, running after the waves that rushed out to sea; and then running back to the safety of her father's arms when the surf rushed back to shore again. And I knew that it was my husband's spirit, as well as his windsurf board, that healed Tommy's soul.

It was time for me to move on and take all those precious memories with me. The best windsurfer on the beach would always be with me, deep in my heart. He was my golden beach boy from so very long ago, my first love, my only love, my Florida Valentine.

BROTHER MIGUEL

by

Patricia A. Stefurak

Bill Donohue was the small town hero of Herkimer, New York. "Willy," as he was called by all his friends, was a scholar and an athlete worthy of being headlined in the "Herkimer Daily" newspaper on a weekly basis. Bill attended St. Lawrence University on a full football scholarship and the town raised the money to purchase his textbooks. Times were lean. He had arrived at the school with only four dollars in his pocket. Soon, Bill surpassed the town's expectations. He won a nationwide essay contest on the topic, "Harry Truman." He got to meet the President, win some prize money, and went on to Europe to read and discuss his essay with European scholars. He graduated in 1938, Suma Cum Laude, with a teaching and coaching position awaiting him at Utica State. Bill was a rugged, handsome, intelligent, young Irishman on his way to conquer the world.

His father, Old Man Donohue, ran the hotel in town and when Bill and his four brothers were home from college or the military, they tended bar in the hotel's basement lounge, a remnant from the speak-easy days of Prohibition. If one of the brothers arrived late to the job, his father pummeled him with his fists and yelled, "You idiot! You stupid boob!" Chances were slim of that brother ever being late again. The Old Man didn't take any crap from his five burly sons, but for some reason the brothers never rebelled, but instead, honored and revered their father.

Bill married his college sweetheart, Mary, and life took them from Utica to Trinidad where he served with the Army Corps of Engineers who were building a military base on this small island. Bill's poor eyesight made him 4F so this was his way of helping with the war effort against Hitler. From Trinidad, the Donohues continued on to Brazil and Peru where Bill became Regional Sales Manager for Sydney Ross, a pharmaceutical maker of aspirin, the miracle drug just being introduced to South America.

June 1958 saw the Donohue family living in Mexico City. It also saw the highly anticipated arrival of a son for Bill Donohue. Although Dad adored his three daughters, a boy had always been his wish. With the birth of Michael, or Brother Miguel, as we sisters affectionately called him, Dad was ecstatic. By this time, he was Vice-President of Latin America for the U.S. pharmaceutical company, Pfizer. We lived the life of Riley: cook, housemaids, chauffeur, gardener, ironing lady, and a membership in the exclusive Club de Golf Chapultepec.

We three girls, Molly, Mary Katherine, and I had always been treated as the boy Dad had longed for. We participated in all sports and were berated if our teams didn't win at all times. The best times were at the Club when we participated in the special holiday races: sack, spoon, the easy no-pressure races. At the end of an afternoon of fun and games, the announcer would broadcast over the loud speaker, "Ladies and Gentlemen, the Donohue girls have done it again! First places in all age categories!" Dad beamed with pride. He loved us and praised us. We'd be giddy with happiness. However, as always, our giddiness was short-lived. At age ten, after an event when Dad had totally put her down, demeaned her, calling her "a boob and an idiot," Molly came to the conclusion that she no longer wanted to do baby races anymore. She quit and she was so thrilled. Soon Mary Katherine and I followed her lead. We decided we'd let our new brother step into the sporting spotlight.

We watched Brother Miguel and waited through his falls, scrapes, tears, and whines until he finally came "of age." It happened the day he learned to ride his little two-wheeler. As he rode away, he turned his head to look back at us, bike wobbling, and beamed such a smile of fulfillment and pride. That smile would stay with me for the rest of my life.

As he got older, Mike began playing baseball. He'd throw that damn ball onto the large awning over my bedroom window for hours and then run and catch it on its way down. From the catch he'd run to an imaginary base and tag the runner out. He was now pitching, catching, and running, doing it all for his one man team.

The next step was Little League. Mike couldn't accept the fact that he wasn't allowed to pitch, run to short stop, catch the ball, and then run to first to tag out the runner. He knew no one could do all this but him. Dad had told him so. After a long talk with the coach, Mike became the pitcher and *only* the pitcher for his team, becoming his team's MVP in this position. The little Irish lad had made it big time and Dad was beyond proud.

Mike left home at age thirteen to attend the prestigious Tabor Academy in Massachusetts, a school with an undefeated baseball team. He excelled in his classes and made the team in his freshman year. He returned to Mexico for holidays and summer vacations and regaled us with all his roguish pranks. Scholastics and sports aside, Mike ran a bookie operation betting on just about anything, and he also hustled money from his dorm mates by playing poker. He said that gave him a few extra bucks for a couple of beers on the weekends.

By 1976, our parents had climbed the social ladder and were now hosting many catered events at home. The head caterer, Bustamonte, loved being in the kitchen listening to Mike go on in flawless Spanish about all his misadventures in the U.S. For these great times, Bustamonte would leave a few "cuba libres" at the table for Mike, who'd sneak up the back steps and proceed to get on a nice teenage "buzz."

Mike graduated Tabor with honors and a full baseball scholarship to Rollins College in Florida. Bright, well read, handsome, bilingual, gifted as a debater on most subjects, funny and friendly, Brother Miguel had life by the tail. He liked the idea of Rollins because it was small and, obviously, had a fantastic baseball program. But mostly, he liked the idea of being able to buy beer at any convenience store in the state. Practices were brutal in the Florida heat. Mike put in one hundred percent plus at every practice and thrived on this hard work. The coaches and team members couldn't believe the arm on this boy. Opening day arrived and as Mike released the first pitch, he knew immediately by the excruciating pain that he'd thrown his arm out.

The phone calls started from Mexico. "You idiot! What the hell did you do? Get it fixed! Here's the name of the best Sports Medicine surgeon in Orlando. Call him and get it fixed! You stupid, stupid boob!"

However, the nerve damage to Mike's elbow was not correctable. His baseball career was over. That part of his life would never be returned to him. The tension with Dad made summer vacations and holidays at home unbearable for Mike, so he remained in Florida and worked at Disney.

Overall, life was still good for Brother Miguel. He was having a great time at college and still had terrific grades and tons of friends. After graduation, he took a job with the state, in charge of a program overseeing welfare recipients. He traveled a lot, visiting his clients at their homes to make sure their food stamps were being used efficiently. He loved hanging out with some of his welfare cases and would always bring along a few beers to share.

After awhile, Mike began to take an occasional trip back to Mexico to visit again. By this time, Dad had settled down and loved having Mike home. They both knew every baseball, football, and basketball stat and the name of every player past and present. You name it, they knew it. They bet on all the games and shared many a cocktail together. The Irish Lad and his Dad. Their conversations ranged from Cervantes to Mickey Spillane, Kant to Emerson, Liberals to Conservatives, red to black. Mike always posed questions that stimulated a lively debate with Dad where tempers would often flair and then, the drinks would again easily flow.

As the years went along though, Mike returned less and less to Mexico. He lost his interest in the art of debate. Now, whenever he would visit, Mike simply stated the facts the way he saw them. His attitude became, "Take it or leave it!" Poker games also became a chore with him playing. Dad would yell, "You boob, why wouldn't you fold with such a shitty hand? You're such an idiot, you screw up the whole game!" Then he'd add, in his best Irish brogue, "I'm pourin', who needs a refill?" By then, we *all* would.

As fate would have it, Molly, Mary Katherine and I all ended up living in Florida with our families. We kept in touch throughout the years and had great times reminiscing about the "good ol' days" in Mexico City. Infrequently, we'd have family get-togethers. I'd phone him, "Hey Brother Miguel, what's happening? Come on over. We're having a cook-out. Afterwards, we'll play some poker."

Mike had always dressed well, but as time went on, his shirts always looked like he'd retrieved them from the pile in the back seat of his car, where he kept several changes of clothes along with numerous cans of beer. He seemed prepared for all contingencies.

One time Mike arrived on a scooter, no license and a six pack in hand – he'd had his first DUI. We all knew Mike was a serious drinker, but so were we. We just thanked our lucky starts that we had never ended up with DUIs. Luck of the Irish!

At future gatherings, Mike arrived in a car driven by one of his "young lovelies." He had a woman in every city and they couldn't do enough for him. He progressively became more and more obnoxious, issuing slurs against women and filthy innuendos about people in general. It finally got to the point when we'd all be fighting with him, but we still allowed him to pour, drink, and serve the liquor. He refused to leave until he'd had the last nasty word and then headed off with one of his lovelies, harassing her as she drove them away. "You idiot," we'd hear him yell, "watch where the hell you're going!" Each of his women thought she'd be the one to finally make him straighten out, that she would be the one who could definitely change his behavior.

Now in 2011, Bill and Mary have passed on and we sisters are all happy with our families and our day-to-day lives. Mike has not fared as well. His slide into alcoholism destroyed his life. He is behind bars for DUI manslaughter.

I visit him and I look away from the remorse and anguish on his face. I see only that little boy, his head turned, bike wobbling, beaming that beautiful smile of pride and joy, of sheer happiness. My mind feels like it's screaming, "Oh, Brother Miguel, what have you done to yourself? You were never, ever a boob!"

SPECIAL DELIVERY

By

Robert J. Dockery

I sat on my front porch nursing a cup of fresh brewed hazelnut coffee with cinnamon sprinkled on top. This was the fateful day. If the check from my last job didn't come soon, my boarders and I would soon be on the street, our butts plopped on the curb with our belongings piled around us.

The letter carrier came at her usual time, driving up in her blue trimmed truck to open my mail box and stuff it with all sorts of junk mail. With a wave and a smile I hollered, "Hi, Dianne. Great weather huh?"

"Good morning to you Mr. K."

She called everybody by their first initial. We had two Mr. Ks on the street. The other one lived three doors down on the opposite side. He's K-E-R-K. I'm K-I-R-K. We're both "Walter."

I checked the weather report on my smart phone. Sunny and hot. Showers late in the day. Another Florida scorcher. About the time I finished my coffee and walked out to collect the mail, Dianne was coming back, delivering to the other side of the street, the odd numbers, Walter Kerk's side. My flip-flops slapped the concrete driveway, a comforting and familiar sound. Like the businessman who clicks his leather heels on a marble floor, it was my way of telling the world to go to blazes.

I got to my mail box about the time Dianne arrived opposite my house. She leaned forward and looked in my direction. "Hey Mr. K. I forgot to tell you. You have a letter that was mailed a really long time ago. It was still in your box this morning. You must of missed it."

"You mean already in the box when you opened it today?"

She nodded. "Yesterday was my day off, so my substitute must of delivered it. I put it on top of the pile so you'd be sure to see it. It only has three cents postage. That was for like a hundred years ago."

"Three cents. Wow. Thanks for telling me, Dianne. Let me take a look right now." I flipped the door down and fished out the mail. The envelope that Dianne had called to my attention sat atop a pile of bills and catalogs addressed to me and to the other people who lived in the house with me.

I studied the handwriting on the envelope: straight, cramped, perfectly formed letters. My brother Tommy wrote that way. He'd been dead for some five years. My heart rate picked up. Goose bumps popped out on my arms.

I set the other mail down on the driveway and examined the envelope. It felt flimsy and had blue borders. The return address wasn't my brother's address. He never lived in D.C. The letter carried a three cent stamp just like Dianne said. The letter was postmarked, December 7, 1941.

The handwriting couldn't be my brother's. He wasn't even born in '41. My father would've been a young man. He used big loops to start the sentences and had a slant that Ma said meant he could have been a famous actor if he hadn't been killed. Nobody ever told me how he died. The writing looked more like my grandfather's. I'd seen a few letters he wrote.

My mother's aunt and uncle raised me after mom died. They never liked dad's side of the family. Never told me much about them except to say dad was rich. I think they were angry when they found out my father left everything to a charity, leaving me and mom with a small trust that went to the same charity when I was 18.

They did tell me that my grandfather was in the navy. Commanded a destroyer Aunt Betsy once told me. "His boat sank with all hands after a torpedo hit it," she'd said.

I realized the mail truck hadn't moved. Feeling eyes on me, I glanced up. Dianne had come out of her truck and stood watching, a look of anticipation in her face. "It's really old, isn't it?"

"Sure is. Must have fallen behind a desk or something and not got found until they remodeled a post office somewhere. I read about that happening."

"You've only moved down from New York a few years ago. How come it's addressed to you here in Florida?"

"That's a great question, Dianne. Let's see. Hmm. My great uncle's name was Walter too. He used to own this house. He didn't have any kids, so when he died, he left everything he owned, including the house, to my mother. Rented it out until I decided to semi-retire and move down here."

"But if he was your mother's brother, his name wouldn't have been Kirk."

"He was my father's brother. Story I got from Aunt Betsy is that he was pissed at his brother for leaving his estate to charity instead of to his family. Uncle Walt never married."

"You're confusing me," Dianne said. "I got to get back on my route." She waved goodbye. "Might be someone's playin' tricks on you."

I picked up the bills and the catalogs and shuffled back to the porch, avoiding my usual flip-flopping as if it might be somehow disrespectful of my precious cargo.

Sarah, one of my boarders, had come out and sat in the glider. Age hadn't erased all of the beauty that made her a successful photography model when she was young. She had on the blue terry cloth robe she wore most days over a blouse and skirt. Her short, athletic body rocked slowly back and forth, the motion creating the little squeaks and groans that I had come to associate with the ancient porch glider. She flashed me a broad toothy smile and said, "You flirtin' wit' Dianne again, Walter?"

"Got a strange letter." I put the junk and bills on the table next to the glider and waved the letter at her. "From my grandfather. Used to be in the navy. Always imagined him a submariner. Nobody knows what happened to him. His boat never came back from a cruise. Most likely got blown up. Maybe it was like in that Clark Gable movie, you know, the Bungo Straits where all our subs got sunk."

"Your grandpa, huh?"

"Yep. Mailed in nineteen and forty-one."

Sarah laughed and slapped her knee. "They ain't kiddin' when they call it snail mail, are they?"

I sat beside her, my heart still racing, feeling a little giddy, the letter from my grandfather held tight between my fingers like it might be some fragile thing. Sarah stared at me a while before she said, "Well. Ain't ya gonna open it? Find out what it says?"

I examined the envelope. It was one of those old letters that are actually part of the envelope. You wrote the letter and then folded it up so it formed the envelope. You wrote the address on the outside. Saved weight for air mail. I would need to be really careful about opening it. Using my finger, I might tear it. Then it'd be difficult to read without putting it back together.

"Think I'll go in and have some breakfast right now, Sarah. Maybe read it a little later. Been around since '41. I don't suppose a few more minutes'll make a difference." I stuffed the letter in my shirt pocket.

"Reckon you're right there, Walter. Strikes me it's like a bottle of fine wine. Might could be better to live with the hopin' rather than pop the cork and find the wine's changed."

Inside the house I joined the three other people who shared it with Sarah and me. There was Jeb Fischer. We called him, Doctor Pepper, because he dressed like a college professor and because of his unruly pepper-and-salt hair. Kate and Hector were brother and sister. Neither of them had married. They were younger, in their fifties.

When I sat down at the table, I popped the letter out of my pocket for a moment so everybody could see it. "Got a letter here addressed to me that was mailed a really long time ago."

"Looks old," Kate said.

"It is old, Kate. Mailed in nineteen and forty-one."

Doctor Pepper said, "I remember those envelopes. I bet it's got the words "air mail" on it too."

"You'd win that bet," I said.

Doctor Pepper craned his neck to get a closer look at the envelope. He chuckled way down in his throat. "Must be important." Then he got a weird look on his face, his lips pursed and his brows knotted. He made his eyes into slits. "Wait just a darn minute, Walter. You're puttin' us on. That's not an envelope. It's a folded letter sheet. No way that could be just now delivered.

You found it somewheres."

Hector jumped up and hollered, "Read it to us. Read it to us."

In a fit of exasperation I shouted, "All right. I'll read it." Sarah, who had followed me into the house, produced a letter opener from her robe pocket and handed it to me.

Her ever-present smile displayed rows of brown teeth. She had no money for the dentist. I swore that if I ever became rich, one thing I'd do first off is get her a new set of teeth so she could be pretty again. Fat chance that, when I couldn't even keep the house.

About then I remembered I'd forgotten to look for the check. I reached over and tore through the stack of mail that Sarah had dropped on the table. No check. My boarders undoubtedly thought I was crazy. They didn't know they were about to be evicted.

I closed my eyes and took a deep breath. My hands trembled. With the greatest care, I gently slid the opener under the flaps and unfolded the letter sheet. My four companions pressed in behind and beside me. I read aloud.

"Walter, my boy. I write to tell you that by the time you receive this, I am on my way to take command of a warship. I do not expect to survive the hostilities. Therefore I want to tell you of the family secret that has been handed down by the men in our family for generations. The women are never, never, told. When your father's plane was shot down in France, it fell upon me to be your advisor in these matters. Knowledge of the secret has been the source of our wealth since our forebears stumbled upon it many years ago. I promise to post a further letter that will describe for you all that you need to know."

The rest of the letter contained a few impersonal comments on the nature of war and its causes. I quit reading aloud, believing it was of no interest to anyone present.

Doc complained that he couldn't see the writing without his spectacles that were upstairs on his nightstand. He didn't feel like going all the way up to his room to fetch them what with his bad leg and all. Sarah read it for me.

In very tiny writing along the edge of the letter, granddad had written something illegible with all the words seeming to run together. I could make out only my name.

Kate said, "It must be a pirate's treasure map."

"It's written in invisible ink," Hector declared in a loud voice as if to force us to believe the truth of the statement.

Sarah said, "Nope. Both wrong. That stuff only happens in stories. Might could be a bank account number."

Doc said, "You never told us you was rich, Walter. Just how much money you got?"

"Well duh! I never got told the family secret, did I, so I never been rich."

"Oh yeah. Right. We'll have to wait 'til he writes you again."

Sarah said, "Then you can let us all live here free 'cause you won't need any more money."

"Wait a darn minute. This letter is a trillion to one shot, like getting struck by a bolt of lightning when the sky is clear blue. If my grandfather wrote me any more letters, what makes you think lightning could strike again? Don't you all think that would be too much coincidence?"

I realized I had at least one sane person in the group when Sarah said, "Might could be."

When I'd re-folded the letter and put it back in my pocket, Doc pointed at me and waved his finger. "Like to have that stamp for my collection." I gave him my version of a withering stare. "When you're done with it, of course. Didn't mean right this second."

For the rest of the day and all day Sunday, the conversation centered around my letter and whether I might be getting more letters. Speculation on what might be the family secret ran rampant with each outrageous suggestion topped by a still more outrageous possibility. The cook even joined in, "Walter must be related to British royalty. As a 'royal' he will get a huge pension." Our cook, whose name was Hanna Heilbronner but who we all called "Cook," hazarded a timid guess that it might be near a million dollars.

I said, "Is that a million a week, a month, a year, or maybe altogether? Anyhow it's Pounds and not Dollars." She closed her mouth and dropped her head and quickly left the room. I felt bad for putting her down. But I was darned sick of my assumed wealth being the main topic of conversation.

By Monday morning things were out of control. I felt stupid being treated as a newly minted rich guy, especially since I was still as poor as ever. My boarders began addressing me as "Sir Walter" and bowing when I entered a room. At table they passed the food to me first and with exaggerated flourishes.

A guy can dream, even if he thinks the dream'll never come true. I was of two minds on the matter and really didn't want to let loose of the idea of coming into great wealth. That's probably why I got annoyed at Hector for suggesting that the letter really was meant for Walter Kerk who lived down the street. "That Walter's been in his house since he was born," Hector said. When I told him to just mind his own business because my Uncle Walter used to live in the house, he said, "Yer a dummie of the worst kind."

"And what does that mean smart guy?"

"Hah! Hah! *El stupido.* Ain't no way ya could be the right guy the letter was sent to. It's fer Walter Kerk and ya know it. Yer *el stupido.*"

I picked up a lamp off the side table next to the sofa and pretended I was about to toss it at him. He ran and hid behind his sister, hunkering down and peering out at me from behind her skirts like a little kid.

I couldn't stay angry at Hector. But I couldn't let him think he got one over on me either, so I said, "Think what you want, Hector. When I find out the family secret and get rich, there's no way I'm going to share it with you. Everyone else'll get some but not you." He made a sad face and tears welled in his eyes. My imagined riches were making me a jerk.

Hector's hectoring got me to thinking. Might be that he was right. Might be that Walter Kerk was the intended recipient of the letter after all. I looked again at the address. The "i" could be an "e". I found no dot above what I had taken initially to be the letter "i". The mind can play tricks. After all these years the dot may have faded.

The street number was definitely 1974. Dianne had read it that way. But was it? I took it under the lamp and examined it closer. The last number began to look a bit like a European 7 with a cross stroke instead of like a sloppy 4. The numeral 1 had a little flag like the Europeans use sometimes. I'd been told that Walt Kerk's mother was originally from Germany. Perhaps it was the Kerk family with a secret that could make Walter Kerk rich. I took out the letter and read it again.

The whole crew was sitting around. Sarah lounged on the sofa reading a new romance novel she'd bought for a dollar in the used book sale at the library. Hector and his sister played a child's board game. Doc sat at the dining table studying his stamps with a large, round magnifying glass. Sitting there in his tattered and threadbare smoking jacket, he looked like Sherlock Holmes down on his luck.

"Hey Doc. Can I borrow that glass a minute?"

He looked up from his work and stared dumbly at me for a while before he chuckled and said, "You want to look at the old stamp I suppose. Remember you promised it to me, so don't you go startin' your own collection now."

He wanted me to confirm that the stamp was indeed to be added to his collection. I wasn't in a bantering mood. So I stood across the table from him and locked my gaze on his lidded, rheumy eyes. He held the magnifying glass close for what seemed like five minutes before he held out his hand and let loose of it.

I took the glass, thanked him, and retired to the ottoman where the light was better. By that time all eyes were staring at me. My boarders knew something was brewing and were eager to know what new and exciting fact I'd discovered.

Upon closer scrutiny, I concluded that the tiny writing at the bottom of the letter might be in German. The German's use those great long words.

My cell phone rang its irritating default jingle that I kept meaning to change. I fished it out of my pocket and looked to see who might be calling. Walter Kerk.

"Hey, Walt," I said. "So good to hear from you. We haven't run into each other for a while. How are you?"

"Good," he replied.

"Happy to hear it. What's up?"

"I hate all this heat, don't you?"

"I get used to it. What's up?"

"I have a letter that might be for you. The mail girl delivered it this morning. She doesn't seem to mind the heat. Our names are so much alike and . . ."

"Yeah. Yeah. Did you open it?"

"No. Misplaced my spectacles. I'm blind as a bat without them."

"How'd you know it's for me?"

"Must be. Damn. Wish it would rain. We could use some rain."

"We sure could, Walt. Why must it be for me?"

"Only mail I get is advertisements and catalogs. I can tell by the feel of it that it's something personal. You know, like flimsy, like a love letter. It has a colored border sort of." He giggled. "You expecting a love letter Walter?"

"Matter of fact I am expecting just such a letter. Thanks for calling."

"Not surprised. Thought it must be for you. I haven't got a real letter in at least ten years, not even a Christmas card. You remember last Christmas when we thought it might snow, it got so cold? Nearly killed my bougainvillea."

It might not have been Christmas for Walter Kerk, but if the missive turned out to be the one I was expecting, it might be Christmas for me and my boarders.

In no mood to make small talk about the weather, I said, "Be over in a couple minutes to pick it up. Thanks," and ended the call.

The instant I returned the phone to my pocket, Sarah, who by then was sitting on the edge of the sofa, the closed book on her lap, said, "He got your letter. The one tells you how to be rich."

"He has a letter Dianne delivered to him by mistake. It's only a letter. Don't get your hopes up."

I handed Doctor Pepper back his magnifying glass. He took it with a smile and said, "You won't be needin' that stamp now."

His obsession with the stamp was getting on my nerves. But I'm basically an understanding guy. Instead of saying something sarcastic, I shook my head and replied, "Got to see what's in the second letter before I can give it to you. I got to take a little walk across the street. Be patient."

Walter Kerk sat on his front porch in his pajamas, chewing an unlit cigar, the kind you get five-in-a-box at the drug store. No smile ever dared invade the downturned mouth or wrinkle the corners of his eyes. In his hand, the hand of a working man, large and rough with thick fingers, he held a letter that had blue borders, looking a lot like the one I received on Saturday.

Walter seldom left his house, preferring to have groceries and other necessities delivered. He did spend a lot of time on the porch. On my walks around the neighborhood, I often took a moment to talk to him. He responded but stayed cool and aloof. Never did he invite me in or even to have a seat in one of the rusted chairs that stood in a neat row, each exactly the same distance from its nearest mate. I would stand on the sidewalk and we would talk about the weather, always the weather.

"Another scorcher," he said and fell silent. I thought for a moment he might be referring to the letter he held out in front of him and waved slowly back and forth.

I approached tentatively, not knowing exactly what he expected of me. At the bottom of the old wooden porch steps, I stopped. He glowered at me. In my best neighborly tone I said, "Weatherman says it'll cool off this afternoon. Expecting a front to move through, bring some rain."

He grinned. "Found my specs right after I talked to you. It ain't for you. It's for me. So you just go on home."

"Now wait just a darn minute, Walt. I'm expecting a letter just like that one. I know it's for me. Just because you never get any personal mail doesn't give you the right to take mine. You know that taking my letter is a federal offense. You can go to jail."

He grinned, waved a dismissive hand and said, "Get outta here 'fore I call the cops." I figured he meant it. The old fool was stupid enough to do that.

I decided to retreat. The letter wasn't going anywhere. He probably planned on building a shrine for it with flowers and candles. His first real letter in ten years. In a way I couldn't blame him for wanting to keep it.

Back at the house, I told my companions what had happened and asked them for ideas how to find out the content of the second letter, the one I believed held the key to my fortune. Hector's response was immediate and somewhat unexpected.

"That old fart Walter will be the rich one. Not fair. That smelly old fart don't scare me. One punch and he's out, and I get the letter."

I appreciated Hector's willingness to go to battle for me. Of course I couldn't let him pound on Walt. I told him, "We can't go around hitting people, Hector."

Doc said, "How about when he's not home we sneak in and take the letter. We can leave one in its place that looks kind of like it. With his bad eyesight he'll never know we switched."

"No good, Doc. He found his specs. And we can't actually steal the letter, only read it. Remember, Dianne did deliver it to him. Besides, he never leaves home."

"No problem," Sarah said. "One of us lures him out of his house. The rest of us go in and find the letter."

"Whom did you have in mind as the lurer?"

Sarah laughed. With a circular motion of her shoulders, she shook off her robe and let it slip to the floor. She unbuttoned the top two buttons of her blouse and pushed out her bosom. She pinched her 64 year old cheeks and shoved her long hair back from her face to tuck it behind each ear. Her skirt she hiked to the knees. The transformation proved to be quite extraordinary.

I said, "OK. Sarah gets the job of lurer. We're a democracy. Anybody opposed?"

A dead silence followed, during which I am sure we all tried to digest what Sarah had just agreed to as her role in our little caper. Hector broke the silence with a loud "Yeah. Right on." The rest of us joined in with clapping and shouts of encouragement.

Doc surprised the hell out of me when he shouted, "Take it off. Take it all off." Sarah advanced toward a red faced Doctor Pepper with a slow, hip-grinding walk.

I concluded that she was more than up to the task of lurer. Old Walt wouldn't know what hit him. His only pleasure for the past how many years most likely consisted of nodding off with Victoria Secret catalogs propped on his pillow. He was a goner for sure.

Cook, who had entered the room sometime during the conversation, shouted, "Hurray for Sarah." She knew Walter Kerk and sometimes cooked for him. However, I was certain she had no idea what was going on so didn't worry about a security breach.

The rest of the day was occupied with in-depth discussions of what Sarah might need to offer to lure Walter Kerk away from his home long enough for us to find the letter. Doc surprised me again and again with his lurid instructions on the art of seduction. Hector concentrated on mapping out a plan for the search. He insisted that we begin in the kitchen because that's where his mother opened letters.

The next morning, Sarah came down to breakfast dressed in a red skirt and white blouse with the three top buttons open. The clothing fit tight about her hips and bodice. Hector couldn't take his eyes off the sheer fabric of her tight blouse. "That will do it. That will definitely do it," he repeated again and again.

Sarah had put on bright red lipstick. Her eyes were shaded, her eyelashes longer, so that her eyes looked bigger and set deeper.

She had tied up her hair in a bun reminding me of the German housekeeper my friend Moises had when we were kids. I thought I smelled Doc's cologne. I'd never seen Sarah made up before. She looked ten years younger and came across as quite pretty. She would have no trouble seducing Walter Kerk.

"Wish me luck, guys," she said. We followed her out to the porch.

"You go girl," the usually quiet Kate advised. In silence we watched Sarah saunter down the street. Her ample backside swayed, defying the laws of gravity and questioning the laws of decency. She crossed the road and climbed the steps to Walter Kerk's porch. He sprang from his chair and reached out a hand to her.

The plan was for Sarah to convince Walter to take a stroll around the block and join her for breakfast at the local pancake house.

Pretending to not be interested in what transpired between Sarah and Walter, we kept a close eye on the proceedings. After sitting for almost a half hour, the two of them got up and headed down the road in the direction of the pancake house.

The game was afoot. The instant the two rounded the corner, Doc said, "Let's roll." He shot down the steps and strode off with a gait that belied his 75 years, not a hint of his usual limp. The reticent stamp collector had morphed into a leader.

Hector shouted after him, "Wait, Doctor. How do we get in?"

Doctor Pepper froze in mid stride. He turned and shuffled back to us, his head bowed, his mouth turned down. He seemed to be confused. "What do we do next, Walter?" he asked, looking up to meet my gaze. So much for our new leader.

"Hector will go in through a basement window. He can go up and open the front door for us."

"No basement," Hector said. "Flood plain. Nearly all of Tarpon Springs is in a flood plain. You got a plan B?"

There was no plan B. There really was no plan A either. We never discussed much beyond Sarah getting Walt out of the house. She concentrated on the luring part, leaving the other details to the rest of us. Stalling, I said, "Well, yes I do, Hector."

Doc spoke up and rescued me. "He uses ventilation screens in the first-floor windows. Hector just climbs in. We boost him up."

I decided it was time for action. "Show of hands," I said. "We go with Doc's plan." Hector raised his beefy hand in a tight fisted salute. Kate raised her hand. "Doc?" Dr Pepper raised his. "OK, the motion passes."

Kate opted to stay behind, explaining that any well-planned caper required a lookout. I wondered exactly what a lookout might do under the circumstances but didn't want to get into that with her. The three of us headed across the street.

Once inside Walter Kerk's house, we found a neat and orderly array of ancient furniture. The place was spotless. Walt must have spent all day cleaning and polishing. Everything'd been detailed, from the nooks and crannies of the kitchen to the highly polished floors.

Hector headed immediately for the kitchen with Doc following him. I spied an envelope with a blue border on a small table by the front door. I snatched it off the table and joined my companions in the kitchen. "What's that noise?" Doc asked.

"Which noise?" Hector said.

"The bell. Sounds like somebody ringin' a school bell like Cook does at dinner."

"Forget it. Let's concentrate on business," I said. "We need to read the letter. We have lots of time. I can take a picture of the letter with my phone. We'll put it back exactly where I found it. Walt won't suspect a thing."

"You leave the letter and he'll know how to get rich too," Doc said.

"True. But we'll know before him."

I took a seat at the little Formica-topped breakfast table on one of the chrome legged chairs. Hector and Doc joined me. "Read it out loud for us," Hector said. Doc nodded in agreement.

I heard talking that seemed to be coming from the back yard. Doc heard it too. "It's Sarah. They're back already."

"No way they had breakfast in that short time," I whispered. "Something went wrong."

I scooped up the envelope and made a run for the foyer with Hector behind me pushing and Doc in the rear. I tossed the envelope onto the table. The three of us ran out the front door and all the way back home, giggling like school children caught misbehaving in the cloakroom.

Kate greeted us on the porch with school bell in hand. Cook stood at her side.

Kate said, "Told you we needed a lookout. I rang the bell soon as they rounded the corner headed this way. Lucky for you they went around the back of the house."

"Thanks Kate," Doc said between gasps. "You done well."

Soon as I caught my breath, I said, "Sarah was laughing like a schoolgirl. Doc, what do you think happened?"

"No idea. Would of thought she might be a mite tense knowin' we was in the house."

"Know what I think?" Cook said.

"No. What you think, Cook?" Doc asked.

"I bet you anything the two of them are over there makin' a good old time right now. You men are all the same. All you can think is how horny the guy is. You forget that Sarah ain't had a date in years. She's hornier than that old man ever was. And I should know."

Hector laughed. "Good for Sarah," he shouted.

"If only I had known," Doc said, a note of sadness in his voice. "I spent too much time buried in my stamp collection." He suddenly jerked his head up and stared at the ceiling. "Come to think of it, I recall a couple times she came on to me. You remember the mistletoe incident last Christmas?"

I had little interest in discussing Doc's sex life. Guys his age ought not to be preoccupied with it.

Sarah didn't come home until nearly six. She wore a toothy smile so wide that I thought for a moment the ends of her mouth had split.

"I never knowed Walter was such an interesting man," she said. "We played checkers and drunk fuzzy navels. He wants to take me to the movies tomorrow. And besides, he's not German. He's Irish. Told me all about how he's part of a long line of infantrymen. Nobody in the navy. So your letter's probably meant for you after all. Strange as that might could be."

Lonely old Walter Kerk had discovered his fortune. It had nothing to do with money.

"Why'd ya come back so quick?" Hector asked.

"Oh. That. I'm really sorry about that. The pancake place was closed."

"I'm happy you two hit it off on your first date," I said. "Did he say anything about the letter?"

"Oh. That. He showed it to me. It was from some vacuum salesman. Tricked out to look like an old air mail envelope. Not a personal letter after all."

The news made my heart sink way down to my toes. It was as if somebody had just dropped me off the top of a tall building.

Hector said, "Glad I didn't go out and buy stuff. I'd have to take it all back."

"Sorry guys. Maybe someday the second letter'll come. Let's be optimistic."

I took the first letter out of my pocket and handed it to Doc. He studied it for a moment and then let out a whoop like a crazed New York Rangers fan.

"What is it Doc?"

"The stamp. The stamp. The stamp."

"Take a deep breath. You're sounding like Hector. Slow down. Tell us what it is about the stamp that's got you all charged up."

"Your granddaddy ever work in a place they print stamps?"

"Aunt Betsy said something about him being a printer when he was younger. Maybe she said something about stamps. Don't recall exactly. Why?"

"The six cent eagle and shield air mail stamp came out in 1938."

"So? What's the big deal?"

Well, the one on your letter is in three cent denomination and says 'air mall' instead of 'air mail.' It was a big mistake, worse'n the old upside down Curtis Jenny biplane stamp. Collectors been whisperin' about this stamp. I always figured it was one of them urban legends they talk about."

"You're saying my grandfather had sticky fingers."

"Not at all. Legend has it that the government sold a few of the stamps before the mistake was discovered."

Hector laughed. "At least one honest person in your family."

I ignored the remark.

"The Jenny is worth a cool million. Philately speaking, this cover will be worth more, a lot more."

That brought a collective gasp.

"Let me see that, Doc." He held it out to me. In a trembling hand, I took the letter.

With a loud smack, I kissed it and raised it up at arm's length like a victorious gladiator might raise a sword. "We can keep the house."

LITTLE SEA WOLVES

by

Trish Commons

"The curtains!"

"The curtains?" I questioned while wiping sudsy sink water from my dripping hands onto my stained apron.

"Just close them!" Babcia hissed, with squinted eyes and a sour smile on her wrinkled and weathered face.

The sounds of horses' hooves and loud rumblings of an overloaded wagon invaded our dwelling. Then another wagon passed. Jewish smugglers were carrying their usual male merchandise of army deserters or political outcasts and their families across the border. Simply strangers in a strange land with just a pittance to live on. The locals called them "little sea wolves."

Our Polish village, Mlawa, brimmed over with these young outsiders from the heart of Russia in 1919. As my fingers parted the worn kitchen curtains, I peeked out our front window. I heard the heavy wheels of a third wagon. A dark shadow of a man sprang out of the back end. His body rolled and tumbled like a river rock caught in a wave of dust.

"Henka, get away from there." Babcia scolded me as she blew out the kitchen's kerosene lamp making the inside of our cottage turn black.

The next morning the smells of fried sausage permeated the air and my stomach growled with a newly awakened interest. I resisted and curled even deeper into my worn knit blanket. Suddenly, I heard a moaning sound outside my bedroom window. The noise came from the backyard. Maybe it could be that stray feline that always scattered the kitchen trash, consisting mostly of potato scraps, across our backyard.

I didn't have time to think since my grandmother began yelling at me to stop being a lazy child. She never gave me any credit. I tied her multi-colored cloths, didn't I? I went to the market in the center of town everyday, didn't I? I smiled at wrinkled and gap-toothed men who leered at me or foul-breathed women who bargained with me, didn't I?

"Henka! You lazy child, get up! We need to get to town early! My rugs need to sell if you plan on eating something besides cabbage and potatoes," Babcia complained in the direction of the bedroom. I shared the cramped space with my brother, Jarek, who in his usual form hadn't come home *again* last night.

Grabbing my shawl, I made a quick motion towards the toilet and awoke quickly when my exposed bottom hit the frigid metallic circle. Once in our backyard, I took in the thick gray mist stretching its wispy arms across the fields as a muted white streak of light grew with the morning. My eyes came to the heap of garbage leaning next to the side of the house. Across the yard a large cornfield grew next to my grandmother's garden of string beans, potatoes and cabbage. I heard muffled moans again in the cornfield, then I noticed part of a man's foot sticking out from the green stalks of corn.

"Jarek? Is that you?"

"Nyet," said an unfamiliar masculine voice.

"Who are you?" I whispered in his direction.

"Alex . . . uh . . . ander," he said in broken words trying to hold in his pain. A young soldier crawled out into the open air with a miserable attempt to stand up but he looked more like a new fawn wobbling as it balanced its weak limbs.

"You fell out of the wagon last night, didn't you?"

"I not fall. I not enough," he paused and looked at me with anger, "rubles to pay that Jew Glotzer. He said anyone not pay extra . . . Glotzer return you to border guard. Bullet kill you. Not want go back. I leap out. I land hard." He rubbed his neck and shoulders as his eyes winced in pain. Locks of stiff coal black hair shifted and stuck out in all directions as he rolled his head sideways.

I had to giggle since talking to a young man, just a few years older than me, had been rare. The only young male I usually spoke to I now avoided since he smelled like cheap vodka and being drunk.

My parents had died from pneumonia when I just turned two. For fourteen years I had been living under Babcia's roof. I never knew my grandfather. He had run off decades before my birth.

"Well, hiding in my grandma's new corn isn't much safer, you fool! You better run before Babcia finds you."

"Babcia?"

"Grandmother."

"Oh, Babushka!"

Suddenly, his mood shifted, his face turned ashen as he grabbed my forearm, gripping my flesh with his strong as steel fingers. His pleading black eyes peered into mine. I realized that his over six foot physique could overpower my petite frame and now wished for other company outside.

"You . . . must help." He tugged at my arm while attempting with his left hand to pull something tawny brown from the inside of his muddied jacket. Inside the packet, there were a few pictures, a scrawled address in Russian and a strip of an official paper wrapped inside an oil-stained envelope. He held out a passenger ticket to me while releasing his hold. Energy-drained, possibly due to hunger, I watched as he struggled to crouch down with his sore body and sit on the pebbled earth.

"Paid passage. . . Port Hamburg . . . ship to New York," he spoke slowly forming his words with his dirty mouth in a round timid face smeared with filth. "Cousin found work for me at fishing village," he said, while putting the contents back inside the envelope and into his military uniform's pocket.

"In New York?"

"Nyet. Flooreedah."

* * * * *

The sweat dripped off my face as I gathered the itchy rugs we had hung that morning around our makeshift stall in the shopping venue. I threw the leftover merchandise of unsold rolls of handmade carpets onto our wagon at the end of the day. It had been a brisk business day.

I thought about the young man throughout the morning and afternoon hours wondering what he could be doing. He had a gentle smile and maybe would be a bit handsomer after a bath. Would he still be there? What would my brother say when he came home? Well, for now the stranger had become my own little sea wolf.

Earlier that morning, I had hidden the desperate and weary soldier in our small barn without revealing even a shred of his existence to Babcia. With ghostlike stealth, I smuggled scraps of sausage wrapped in a kitchen towel for the stranger. He devoured it. He could not be more than 19 or 20 and had a kind face. I had carried two horse blankets to a nearby corner of hay to create a makeshift bed for him to try and recover his strength during the day. The farm horse, Ginnie, whinnied as if to complain about the use of her blankets as I hurried back outside and to the cottage's kitchen.

"Where were you?" Babcia asked.

"Just taking some old garden carrots to Ginnie out in the barn. She looked more tired than usual yesterday," I lied. "I thought a treat might perk her up. She's not a young filly anymore."

"Well, just hurry and get her hitched up so we can go," Babcia replied.

I played the obedient role of granddaughter the rest of the long day. The familiar cadence of the wagon's wheels often lulled me back to sleep during our journey to the marketplace but not today. The same ritual of passing the same dilapidated dwellings throughout the blocks of homes became more bearable as I thought of my new friend. The tannery always caught my eye with its hides displayed, and within a few minutes we arrived at the market in the center of town, jostling for our spot in the overflowing traffic, overpowering dust and overeager people walking. I hitched up Ginnie next to the same wooden stall we used daily, feeling a bit guilty for not giving her any carrots like I had said. We entered the marketplace in haste like always. Babcia knew most of the other locals from the Polish Catholic church. The other side of the market filled up with Jewish shopkeepers selling leather goods from the popular tannery, deli meats, handmade beaded jewelry, clay pottery and multiple fruits and vegetables. The Orthodox Jews looked so different in their long beards and side curls and black hats. They never smiled at us and we cursed at them under our breath.

Babcia kept a close eye on her wares. She thought every Jew capable of stealing, from the youngest urchin to the devoutly dressed rabbis. She never really trusted anyone, even the priests from her own local parish. Finally, the day came to a much-needed close as the fall sunlight settled across the western hills.

"Don't forget the tarp to cover up those rugs or the rain will surely ruin them."

"Have I ever forgotten? You treat me like such a baby. I do the same thing every day, Babcia. Do you really think I would forget if you didn't remind me again and again?"

"Yes you would because you . . . like your brother, Jarek . . . are lazy children. I am stuck with the both of you."

"I hate you," I said to myself so softly that she couldn't hear. I tried to help her and please her. Today, I would displease her. Served her right. The man's arrival at least had broken up the daily drudgery of my pitiful life.

We loaded the last rug back into the wagon and arrived a few minutes later to our sorrowful dwelling where smells of cooked cabbage wafted through the air.

"Jarek must've started dinner for us. Ah ha, his guilt from never returning last night! If he does not do his load of work, mark my words, I will throw him out!" she remarked loudly, while walking toward the house in her small misshapen female form.

"Henka, unload and unhitch the wagon," she grumbled.

"Yes, Babcia," I stammered out, a bit nervous since I knew the Russian deserter might still be close by.

Entering the musty smelling barn, I saw his blanket over the hay with an indentation where his Russian body must have lain. Maybe he had left for good? I took care of the cargo and settled Ginnie in her stall with fresh hay and water when suddenly I heard loud screaming from the house.

"Get out of here or I'll shoot you! Henka! Jarek, are you here? JAREK!" Babcia shrieked.

"Babushka! Me good. Not hurt," the wayward stranger spoke nervously with an attempt to convince grandmother that no harm would befall her.

"I mean it! I will shoot you! Off my property!"

I could hear her loud tirade of words from outside the opened front door as I ran inside the cottage. High up on his chest, he wore Babcia's apron - soaked in blood. There were drops across the floor and on the table along with the remnants of what looked like wild rabbit's fur. He must have caught it and skinned it. Bits of torn cabbage leaves including its core lay beside it. He had been attempting to cook for us. Steaming meat cooked in a large pot of boiling water next to a black skillet of simmering cabbage.

"Thief! Get out! Get out!" Babcia continued while I took in the scene.

"It's alright. I will clean up this mess. He wanted to help. Look, no harm has been done," I said in soothing tones standing between the sea wolf and my grandmother.

He took off the apron and handed it to me haphazardly smearing blood across my bodice.

"Now, look what you have done to my granddaughter!" Babcia shrieked again. "There's blood everywhere!"

She picked up the knife and continued her loud threats as he exited through the back door in a hurried fashion. I walked behind him but accidentally tripped over the neighbor cat and collapsed on the ground in a tumble.

Just then my still inebriated brother, Jarek, stumbled in and saw the scene before him. He grabbed the knife from Babcia and stabbed the young Russian in the heart with its sharp blade. The stranger gasped and fell back into the cornfield. We buried him that night but only after I said a few words of prayer.

Wanting to flee from my life, I went into the barn to lay on the bed where the stranger's warm body had lain just a few hours before. Next to the woolen blanket's fabric, I saw the brown paper ticket. Without a word, I took the rubles from a pottery jar hidden in the wagon that Babcia thought I never knew about and left to take the Hamburg ship to Florida. I walked silently up the rugged hill towards the railroad station. Now, I would be a little sea wolf.

THE JOURNEY HOME

by

John Dunn

The old man was on his knees, as if praying, when he heard the high pitch of the whistle. "It's time I do it, but I need to be standing up first," he thought.

The whistle continued as he wrapped both hands around a black metal poker and struggled to his feet. Turning, he plodded in the direction of the ever-blowing whistle, as the steam wafted around the corner to acknowledge his destination. Rounding the bend, the man's aged eyes fixed on the loud whistle-blowing steam maker.

When an arm's length away, the old man reached with his leathery right hand . . . and removed the copper kettle from the gas burning stove. "That's enough noise for one night."

Three white ceramic cups and a container of cocoa mix lay on the butcher block countertop. But who were the other two cups for? He couldn't remember. His short term memory had been getting worse over the last year.

Disgusted with his lack of recall, he set the kettle on the counter next to the cups and made his way back to the living room. Once again he grabbed the poker and, leaning no further than necessary, he stirred the glowing red embers. Sparks took flight into the chimney like fireflies in a summer's night air.

Standing his makeshift cane against the stone hearth, the old man turned and meandered around the sofa and antique roll-top desk. He paused at the large bookshelves built into the back wall of the living room, and let his hand glide over the spines of the vast book collection. He began at the upper left corner and moved to the right, then repeated the process at each descending set of shelves, as if a blind person reading Braille. His hand finally stopped. "Ah, here you are." He'd always had a strong reverence for books, instilled in him as a young boy; books not in use were placed back on the shelf, just as in the library.

With the book clutched in his hand, the man headed for his favorite chair, his Nana's rocker. Joe's grandfather built the hardwood rocker for his grandmother when they were newlyweds. She sat in it at night quilting or crocheting by the glow of a fire. Through the years it became necessary to add padding to the seat and back, but Joe never missed a night to sit in that rocker.

Before he could reach the chair, the front door burst open and a young girl and small boy hurried in. "Grandpa, Grandpa, look at the fish we caught in the pond!"

Joe was startled at first, but then smiled and exclaimed, "I told you there were plenty of fish in there!" Behind the children came his daughter Kathy, with the fishing poles, and his son-in-law, Tom, with the catch of the day.

"Joe, the kids had a good time on the pond this evening." Tom headed for the kitchen as he spoke. "While I clean the fish, you kids get washed up. After that you can have your hot cocoa."

Now the old man remembered why three cups were out.

Kathy followed Tom into the kitchen, pausing briefly to kiss her father on the cheek. On the counter she found the cups, kettle, and cocoa mix. She also found something she hadn't expected. The burner on the stove still glowed with the flame her father had forgotten to turn off. Kathy placed the kettle back on the burner to make sure it was still hot. It didn't take long for the kettle to whistle again.

After turning off the stove, she fixed the hot chocolates, then reached into the cupboard above the sink and took down two more mugs for Tom and herself. The children ran into the kitchen and grabbed the cups, then headed into the living room as the hot vapor rose from the drinks. "Be careful, it's hot," Kathy called out. She took a cup to her father and returned to the kitchen. Tom had just finished cleaning the five small Brook Trout and was washing his hands in the sink.

"Tom, he's getting worse. He left the stove burning. Who knows what could be next?"

Tom took Kathy's hands in his. "We've talked about this before. We have plenty of room with us, and the kids would love to have Joe around."

Kathy shook her head, "He'll never leave this place; he loves it here."

"It won't hurt to discuss the situation with him."

Again she shook her head as they returned to the living room. Joe sat in the rocker near the warm fire that helped illuminate the room. The book retrieved from the shelf rested on the maple end table. The two children sat comfortably on a large area rug that partially covered the oak floor.

In between sips, the little blonde haired girl asked, "Grandpa, why do you have so many books?"

Joe fastened his right hand on the antiquated book and setting it in his lap, replied, "I enjoy reading them. They keep me young."

The little boy chuckled. "But Grandpa, you're ooold."

"I may be old on the outside, but on the inside I'm still a young man. Now-a-days I can't physically do what you kids can; however, with a book I can go anywhere and do anything. And I don't need a television or computer, just my imagination," the old man added. "Take this book for example," he said, his hand still attached to the opus. "Robinson Crusoe. With this book I'm sailing the ocean, being shipwrecked on a tropical island, struggling every day to survive."

"That's an old person's book," the little girl said.

"Well, Heather, let's see if we can find a more suitable book for you and Joey." The little boy was named after his grandfather. "Go to the bookshelf," the old man instructed. Joey jumped to his feet and bolted across the room. "Now the third shelf down and to the right there is a bright yellow book. Do you see it?"

Standing on tip-toes, Joey's wee hand latched onto an old thin yellow book. "Is this the one, Grandpa?"

"Read the title," came the reply.

"Cu-ri-ous Ge-orge?" the boy asked quizzically.

"That's the one. Bring it here." Joey handed the book to his grandfather. The old man flipped through the pages with a smile, then gently closed the book and glanced at the children. "Now let me tell you a story. When I was your age my grade school class marched through the halls in single file to the school library. After learning about the Dewey Decimal System, we students were allowed a few minutes to browse through the many books and check two of them out for a week.

"I enjoyed the books so much I didn't want to return them, so of course, I looked forward to the annual book fairs. For several days out of the year the gymnasium was transformed into a book store. Large tables full of books of every size were set up on the wood floor. The first day I would survey the large selection and make my choices, then came the tough part, convincing mom and dad to lend me the money to buy them.

"At night, after a bath and having my cocoa, one of my parents sat at the edge of the bed and read from MY book. Dad merely read the words, but Mom could transport me into the story just by the way she changed the tone of her voice. Then after a good-night kiss, I'd stare out the bedroom window, listen for the nearby train and conjure up stories of my own."

"We have chocolate drinks, Grandpa." Heather raised her cup in the air with both hands.

"Well then, we just need a good story," said Joe. He leaned back in his chair. "I still have all those books from the book fairs. Which one would you like to hear?"

"Let's hear about the monkey!" the two children shouted in unison.

"O.K., Curious George it is," Joe replied with enthusiasm. The children sat on the floor fascinated; hanging on every sentence their grandfather read.

Kathy and Tom sneaked back into the kitchen. "After the kids are in bed we'll have a talk with your father," Tom said, as he put his arms around his wife and gave her a hug. "It'll be alright," he told her. "You'll see." A few minutes later they returned to the reading session that was just coming to an end.

"Grandpa, can you read another one?" Joey asked.

Their mother quickly interrupted, "Not tonight, tomorrow is another day. Give Grandpa a kiss and get ready for bed, it's late."

Both youngsters whined, "Ah Mom."

"You heard your mother," Tom said. Reluctantly they rose from the rug and took turns hugging the old man.

"Good-night, Grandpa," they each told him.

Joe replied, "I'll see you in the morning." As they headed down the hall, Kathy followed to make sure they each took a bath and made it to bed without any horseplay. Tom placed another log on the fire.

When she returned, Kathy sat on the sofa next to her husband directly across from Joe. "Dad," she said quietly, "I know how you love being here in the mountains and living in this cottage, but you're not a young man any longer, and you need someone to help you here."

Joe's reply came gently, "I know you both worry about me being alone, but I'm alright. My back is not what it used to be and I get a little forgetful every once in a while, but when you're my age, you won't be able to remember everything either."

Kathy spoke up with angst in her voice, "Did you know you left the stove on this evening? What about your medication? How many times do you forget to take that?"

Tom could sense his wife becoming more anxious, so he interrupted. "Joe, Kathy and I have been discussing this for a couple of months. We want you to move in with us. With both of us working we can afford to hire someone to be with you during the day, and we'll be home at night. The kids adore you, and it would be good for you as well as them if you were around more."

His head hanging low, the old man gazed at the fire. Without taking his eyes off of the flame he said, "Perhaps you're correct about certain things, but this is where I belong, not Florida."

With tears beginning to well up in her eyes, Kathy told her father, "We all want to spend more time with you. We love you very much."

Joe reached out his hand to his only child. Standing, she leaned over and gave him a hug as he replied, "I know you do, honey, let me think about it." At that instant Kathy knew it was a foregone conclusion. In her thirty-five years, not only had she learned much from her father, but also much about him. That was his polite statement. Anytime he used those words (let me think about it) his mind was already made up. His answer would be no.

The next morning a disheveled Joe shuffled along the wood floor towards the kitchen in his open heeled slippers. His robe hung open revealing a sleeveless "T" shirt and a pair of blue jeans, and his hair awaited a comb to run through it.

Kathy was already busy making breakfast for Tom and the kids; the smell of bacon and toast filled the air. "Good-morning, Dad. Coffee?"

"Where are the kids?" asked Joe.

"They're getting dressed," replied Tom, who was sitting at the table with the paper and coffee.

As he sat down Joe mumbled, "I came to a decision last night."

Kathy stopped what she was doing and leaned against the counter, arms folded, still holding the spatula in her left hand. She was stunned. Her father's usual policy was to avoid issues and put them off in hopes others would magically forget about the subject.

After clearing his throat, Joe continued, "Ah um. I'll allow you to hire a caregiver to come to the house three days a week, but I don't want to move back to Florida."

It wasn't that he thought it was a good idea and that he needed help. On the contrary, he just wanted to get his daughter off his back. She could be relentless in her pursuit to help her father. Her stubbornness was a trait inherited from her mother. Although loving, when Joe's wife set her mind on something, she wouldn't let it go until she got her way. Like the time she found three puppies abandoned alongside Godwin Avenue back in New Jersey and adopted them. Joe had been out of work for two months and there was barely enough money to put food on the table, let alone pay for vet bills and dog food. And the time she insisted the family move to Florida for the warmth, so Joe could work year round at his trade of block mason. No more time off for cold weather.

This was not the solution Kathy wanted, but if Joe wouldn't come to Florida, this must be the next best way. Disappointed she said quietly, "I'll call an agency and see who they have. This way we can choose someone before we leave."

"I'll take that coffee now," Joe said.

Tom picked the paper up from the table and let his eyes glance over the top of the page as he watched his wife rub her forehead with one hand and flip pancakes with the other.

Later that day Kathy made the calls. In such a small town as Boone, North Carolina, there was only Mrs. Baker, a retired nurse who had lived in the town all her life. She was nice enough and had an extensive medical background over the last forty years, as well as being a bit of a local legend as a Blue Ribbon winner of many county fair cook-offs. However, Tom and Kathy had to rule her out.

"Why can't Old Lady Baker be the one to come over?" Joe inquired. "I like her. At least she knows how to cook."

"I'm glad you like her, Dad, but what if you fell? Mrs. Baker doesn't have the strength to help you back up," exclaimed Kathy. "I'll call the Donaldson Agency in Asheville tomorrow."

"Oh don't be silly, that's an hour away. It will cost so much extra for someone to come that far," blurted out Joe.

Two days later, Mrs. Parker, a representative of the Donaldson Agency, arrived. She inquired about Joe's health and medications as well as his likes and dislikes. "I realize there are many questions, but it helps to get as much information as possible so we can match Joe with a caregiver he'll be compatible with. The more comfortable he is the better the results," expressed Mrs. Parker.

After forty-five minutes of quizzing, conversation, tea and cookies, Mrs. Parker stood up and said, "I have the perfect person for you. His name is Matthew. He is a sturdy young man and works for us while going to Medical School right here in town at Appalachian State University. He'll be a nice match for you, Joe. I'll bring him by tomorrow so you can meet him, if that's okay?" Tom, Kathy, and Joe agreed. "Thank you for the tea and cookies. And Joe, you have a wonderful home," said Mrs. Parker.

The next morning Kathy was up early and strolled to the small boat dock extending into the pond next to the cottage. Tom followed a half hour later bringing his wife her blue and pink knitted sweater; the November mountain air was getting cooler with each shortening day. "I thought you might want this." Tom handed the sweater to his wife.

"Thank you," replied Kathy. "We're doing the right thing, aren't we?"

"Under the circumstances, it's about the only thing that can be done. If we force your father to leave here he'll just resent us. And that's not going to help anyone."

"I just hate the thought of being so far away if anything were to happen. I wish he could understand he should be with family now," stressed Kathy.

The husband and wife sat quietly watching a hawk fly overhead searching for a trout swimming in the pond. The rising sun reflected off of the low clouds turning them orange, red, and silver against the bluing sky. Once it crested above the trees, Joey ran out from the cottage and shouted, "I'm hungry. Can we have breakfast now?"

By mid-afternoon, Mrs. Parker pulled her car into the gravel drive. The driveway was a small distance from the home as not to spoil the special feel one gets when seeing a cottage in the woods. She and her protégé walked the slate pathway which skirted the stream that flowed out of the pond. Smoke from the chimney and the glow of the fire through the windows welcomed the guests.

Kathy met them at the door. "Good afternoon, Mrs. Parker. How are you this chilly day?"

"Oh lovely, I'm glad I remembered to bring my jacket."

"Come on in. The fire will warm you up. Please have a seat," Kathy said. "May I offer you some coffee or perhaps a cup of tea?"

Mrs. Parker spoke up first and said, "I'll take tea please, two sugars."

"Coffee, black will be fine, thank you," said the dark haired young man.

"Is Joe at home dear?" Mrs. Parker asked as their hostess made her way into the kitchen.

"He and Tom took the kids for a little hike in the woods. But they should be home soon."

Kathy set the tray of hot drinks on the coffee table; the older woman reached for her cup. "Kathy, this is Matthew, the young man I was telling you about."

"It's nice to meet you."

"Thank you ma'am, and for the coffee as well."

From outside the cottage came a barrage of laughter and carrying on. "That sounds like the gang now," said Kathy. The front door flung open and in marched the two children with their father and grandfather. "Everyone, Mrs. Parker and her friend just arrived."

After the introductions were made all around, Matthew turned to Joe and said "I've been looking forward to meeting you, Joseph." The group of adults had a long discussion as to what Joe expected from Matthew and what he would expect from Joe. On more than one occasion the conversation was sidetracked to how wonderful it must be for Tom and Kathy to live in Florida with the warm weather and beaches. An hour and a half later Mrs. Parker and Matthew said their good-byes with an agreement that the young man would begin tending to Joe the following week.

That weekend Tom, his wife, and the kids packed up and headed for home. Their Thanksgiving vacation was over. They both needed to get back to work and the children back to school. The good-byes were tearful and Joe's daughter was very apprehensive about leaving her father with his deteriorating condition, although he now had a capable caregiver.

"Don't you worry, I'll be fine. You just have a safe trip home. I love all of you," Joe said as he waved good-bye.

Monday morning around ten, Matthew arrived and knocked on the door. "Good morning Joseph, I thought we might get started and sort of get to know each other a little better."

"Come on in," Joe said. "So what do you want to know about this old man?"

"Oh, just start wherever you want."

"Well I was born in northern New Jersey, just across the Hudson River from New York City. It was a bone chilling February morning at the Catholic Hospital, and I was sucking down bottles right and left. One of the Sisters told my father he would have to hold down two jobs just to feed me. Ha, ha! Indeed, Dad did have two jobs. Of course, I wasn't the only reason for his hard work. He wanted a better life for his family than what he had.

"Growing up, my friends and I would build the typical snowman. Walls of snow became forts and tops of garbage cans were used as shields to protect us from the snowballs we would throw at each other." Joe began to squirm around on the sofa. "Ha, ha. The good-ole days."

"What's wrong Joe?" Matthew asked.

"Just some old bones I guess. My arthritis is acting up a little and it's hard to get comfortable."

"So when did you move to Florida?"

"In 1969. That's when Beth, my wife, decided we had to move south. When I took my wedding vows I promised her I would do anything to make her happy. So as much as I didn't want to leave, I granted her that wish. Six years later Kathy came into our lives. Beth couldn't have children, and we both wanted a little girl desperately ever since we were married. So even though we were in our late forties God blessed us with the ability to adopt a baby. Fifteen more years went by until my Beth was called home. I stayed in Florida until Kathy was married and I retired. Then I began a new chapter in my life, and came to where it felt right. The mountains."

"And somewhere along the way you gave your life to the Lord."

"Why would you make a statement like that?"

"You have a collection of Bibles on your book shelf; you wear a cross. And if I were a betting man, I'd say you pray a lot."

"You're right. I grew up in the Church. My mother and father always made sure I was in Sunday school. That's where I met Beth. We were in the children's choir and the youth group; we were best friends and grew up together."

"I also went to church. I did a lot of volunteer work there. Did you ever do any volunteer work?" asked Matthew.

"I would visit my grandfather in the nursing home near the end of his life. I think it made a difference for him that I was there. After he died, I began volunteering for hospice, and tried to make the passing for others easier. Beth always understood."

Finally Joe suggested, "Let's take the boat out on the pond and do a little fishin'." Matthew agreed. The day was cold, but the sun shone bright as it lit the pond surrounded by the tall conifers. The still water reflected the white clouds like a mirror as the two men sat in the small Jon boat, neither one catching a thing.

All of a sudden Joe dropped his fishing pole into the pond and grabbed his chest. Matthew calmly lay down his pole and reached out his right hand and looked Joe in the eye.

"Take my hand, Joseph."

"What's going on?" Joe stretched out his arm.

"It's time for the final part of your journey." Matthew placed his left hand around Joe's back supporting him as he held onto him with his right.

"It hurts real bad!" Joe clutched Matthew's arm.

"The pain will stop in just a minute, and you'll never feel pain again. Just don't let go of my hand. I'll be with you every step of the way." With that, Joe slumped forward, his head resting on the young man's chest.

Matthew began to pray, "Lord, I commend to you your faithful servant Joseph, whose work on earth is through. Accept him Oh Heavenly Father into your Kingdom. I pray this. Amen."

Joe slowly raised his head and sat up on his own. "That was bad. I should go into the house and rest a bit. But for some reason I feel good, totally energized. I could spend the rest of the day fishin'!"

"So we shall!" exclaimed Matthew. After retrieving Joe's pole from the pond, the men went back to fishing. This time they were catching all kinds of fish. "You understand what happened just now, don't you?"

Joe smiled and replied, "I believe I just died, but how come I'm still here on the pond? Did I do something wrong that I can't get into Heaven? I thought I would see Beth when I got there. And you. You seemed to know what I was going through. Are you an Angel?"

"I was with you the day you were born, the day you took your first steps, and the day you said your first hello to Elizabeth. I witnessed your wedding and was there to bring her home the day you said your last good-bye. I've been with you your whole life. You've accepted me as your Lord and Savior and brought me much joy. Your journey home is over. This is your part of Heaven, and Elizabeth is waiting for you at the cottage."

Joe rowed the boat as fast as he could to the little dock. Once out of the boat he looked at Matthew and dropped to his knees and said, "Thank you Lord."

"Go my son."

Joe jumped to his feet and ran to the front door of the cottage where Beth stood waiting.

MY DUNCAN, MY HERO

by

Marge Marante

Finally! It was a beautiful, sunny, pleasantly warm Florida day. As typical for April, the repressive humidity had not yet set in. But the rain. Boy, had we had rain. *What a relief to see sunshine after enduring twelve days of rain,* I thought as I headed to the barn. All the ditches and ponds had overflowed their banks. I was so happy to finally be able to play with Duncan although I was not sure what shape the riding areas would be in. *I sure hope there is a little piece of dry land left.* That was a big wish as in years past, the barn had ended up underwater after a deluge of rain.

Excited, I anticipated seeing my boy, Duncan; my gorgeous, 16 hands, stocky four year old gelding. His coat, a golden chestnut color, had white snowflakes sprinkled over him, especially over his rump. That sure made it easier to spot him in the pasture at dusk. It was like having reflectors on. He was a handsome guy, especially with that wide, white blaze running down his face. And those mischievous, big brown eyes. You could almost see him thinking of ways to get into trouble.

* * * * *

As I pulled up to the barn, the smell of newly blossomed flowers permeated the air. But the sweeter fragrance to me was the aroma of the horse barn. The combination of hay and horses. There was no better smell. I could see the pond in our pasture had overflowed its banks too, covering most of the pasture. My earlier smile, just thinking about getting to play with Duncan, turned to a very definite frown. And to make matters worse, the horse herd had found a way into the neighbor's pasture. *Okay,* I thought. *Now I will have to trek all the way around the edge,* as their pond took up the entire middle of that pasture. Naturally, Duncan appeared at the farthest end and was not about to come to me when I called to him. He was not a dumb fellow and not particularly interested in me putting a stiff saddle on him at the moment, let alone placing my body in it. He much preferred to stay with his buddies, eating the luscious grass, wading and splashing in the cool pond and in short, just hanging out. A submerged pasture was Duncan's utopia. He loved water. He would even roll in the water and all you would were his legs sticking out, swaying back and forth as he rolled under the water. He even would eat grass on the bottom with water coming up to just below his eyes. He learned to hold his breath while he munched.

"Duncan, please come here," I pleaded. "Don't make me walk all the way over there."

He raised his head, kept munching, and watched me struggle to walk a thin path along the side between the fence and the overflowed pond. It was all I could do not to fall into the water on the uneven, slippery ground. Duncan watched for a while, and then went back to grazing, pretty sure I could not get to him.

The water was too deep to cross to his location. I had to climb a fence at the far end to make my way to the other side, to climb back over on his side. I am sure Duncan thought he was safe and that I would never go to that much effort to get to him. *WRONG!* I came back over the fence toward him and he knew he was ha. He reluctantly came over to me.

As I slipped on his halter and lead rope, I pondered how to get us back to the barn. There was the deep pond between us and the barn. No gates out of this pasture. Naturally the one and only gate was totally submerged. My luck. It was evident there was only one way back. *Cross the pond,* I told myself. My mind was trying to determine how I was going to accomplish that.

We walked down the pasture where the pond appeared shallower.

"Okay, boy. We have to cross here. No stopping to splash me," which was his favorite thing to do. Duncan gave me a push with his nose as if to say, "Let's do it then."

"You nut case. If you weren't so damn tall, I'd get on you and ride you across." With me being only 5'2", even with a saddle on him, I needed a two-step stool to get on him. "Okay, let's go." I took a deep breath, not really that concerned. "What's a little water?" I rationalized.

We started across the water and it, indeed, was less deep. But that being said, it was up to my knees. After maybe three steps, I suddenly sank down into the mud with both feet. Duncan continued to walk. I held firm onto the rope. Being that my feet were going nowhere, I was pulled face first into the water.

I came up sputtering. It was then that I realized I was stuck. The more I tried to move my feet, the more stuck I became.

"Great," I muttered to Duncan. "This is not good"

Duncan by now had stopped and turned his head to look at me. I was sopping wet, mired in mud, water up past my knees and unable to move. What a predicament. Without any options, I looked at my surprised horse.

"Duncan, my boy, you've got to get me out of here." Totally dumbfounded as to how I really was going to get out of this dilemma, and truly convinced that Duncan could not do anything, I instinctively clucked to him. Lo and behold, he began to walk. As he pulled, my body went horizontal to the water. He kept walking and my feet finally were pulled out of the muck.

I did not dare to try to stand up and get stuck again. Amazingly, Duncan kept walking, pulling me all the way to the opposite shore. In fact, he pulled me well up on the shore before he finally stopped, turned his head and stared at me. His big brown eyes warmly looked at me as if to say, "Did I do okay, you moron?"

I was never so thankful to have my buddy take care of me. I could not kiss and hug him enough. Once back to the barn, he got treats, accolades and no riding.

When I arrived home, I told my husband of his miraculous feat. "That Duncan saved my life," I burst out so proud of my buddy.

My husband responded, but not exactly how I expected. He replied accusingly, "That horse almost got you killed!"

"What?" I could not believe his reaction. "He was my savior. How can you say that? He was a hero!"

"If you didn't have that horse," he said, shaking his finger at me, "you wouldn't have been in that damn pond in the first place."

Hmmm. He had a point. But Duncan still was my hero.

* * * * *

Weeks later, still glowing from the feat of my hero horse, I puttered around in the barn while Duncan munched to his hearts content in the grass filled paddock. He seemed so happy to be away from the herd for a while. He had all this grass to himself.

I finally finished my chores and went into the paddock to pet him. I suddenly heard dogs barking, the sounds coming from my neighbor's farm. I did not know her dogs but did know of their reputation. They were not nice mongrels. I looked over in that direction and saw three menacing pairs of eyes glaring at me through the wood slats of the fence. Their barking turned into vicious snarls. I realized I was defenseless and needed to get back to the safety of the barn. Thank goodness there was a phone in the barn. This was before cell phones so a phone there was a God send. That is, if I could make it to the barn. And right then that was a big IF.

"Hey, Duncan," I said, my voice starting to quiver. "I think I will back peddle to the barn." Now did I really think he would understand me? Probably not; however, I was pretty sure he sensed how scared I was. I did not dare turn my back on those nasty dogs. One slow agonizing step at a time, I backed toward the barn, knowing I would still have to stop, turn, climb the fence and have another 200 feet to flee to the barn. The sweat now was running down my face as I became really concerned for my safety.

I was not sure I had time to actually make it to the barn, awkwardly backing, but still felt it was better not to turn and run. The dogs were getting closer and I started to panic. I saw Duncan still nonchalantly grazing on that delicious grass. Yet his eyes were watching the dogs and watching me, back and forth. For a fleeting moment, I was concerned about his safety but reassured myself that at 1200 pounds, he could probably fend for himself. On the other hand, I had never seen any aggressive behavior in him. Could he really defend himself? I had no other choice. He would have to take care of himself with whatever was about to happen to us. My heart now pounding out of my chest, fear gripping me, I prayed I would not trip, making a bad situation worse.

The dogs were now past him and gaining on me. *I'm done for,* I thought. At this point, pure terror ensued.

All of a sudden, Duncan picked up his head and tore over to me at a rapid pace, turned facing the three dogs and attacked them at full force. They all took off running back from where they came, yelping as Duncan clipped a couple of them with his hooves, before they could get out of his way.

I just stood there with my mouth wide open in disbelief. He trotted back over to me as if to ask, "How many more times must I save your frickin neck?" Still reeling from this near disaster, I laughed, I cried, and of course, hugged my hero, AGAIN!

* * * * *

Should I tell my husband about this episode? *Probably not!*

THE QUEST

by

Deanna J. Bennett

The man from the Second Chance Shelter took two large black trash bags from Margaret. "Thank you, ma'am," he said. "I know the men at the shelter will appreciate getting these clothes."

"You're very welcome."

With that, Margaret closed the door, leaned her back against it, and wept sad tears, her chest heaving with her sobs. Sam was gone. And so was the last of his clothing. Except for the one blue denim shirt that she couldn't part with. Whenever she reached bottom, missing him so much that she despaired of life, she clutched it tightly to her chest while she cried. She did that less and less frequently over the past two years and had now moved his shirt to the back of her clothes closet. There, but no longer a constant reminder that her husband of thirty-five years was dead.

She wiped her tears with the backs of her hands and gave herself a talking to. She'd always done that, and mostly it worked. *Get yourself together, Margaret. And carry out your promise. You said when the last of Sam's clothes were gone you'd set out on a new life. You're lonesome. All you have to do is find a new man and everything will be all right.*

Margaret picked up the morning's *St. Petersburg Times* and pulled out the want ad section. "Well, what do you think of that!" she exclaimed out loud. "They don't have a section for men wanting to meet women. I used to read that and tell Sam I was shopping for his replacement." Her lips quivered, but she set her jaw, raised her head high, and put the paper down. "How am I going to meet men if there are no want ads?"

"Aha!" She reached for *Creative Loafing*, the free alternative newspaper. They had the best restaurant and movie reviews and information about weekly events. She also knew they had Men seeking Women, and Men seeking Men and all the variations and combinations for both sexes.

"What?" she cried out. "They're gone. How will young male studs find mature male companions? And how am I going to find Mister," her lips trembled and she resolutely pressed them together a moment, "Mister . . . Mister Next."

The phone rang.

"Hello?"

"Hi, Margaret. It's Dorothy. Shirley says there's a great Labor Day sale on bathing suits at Dillards. Want to go?"

"I'd love to go but I don't know about the bathing suit sale."

"Oh, come on. It will do you good to get out. You can always buy a cover-up instead of a suit."

"Well, okay."

"Good. I'll pick you up in 15 minutes. See ya."

* * * * *

Margaret put her handbag on the chair and hung an armload of swimwear on the hook in the dressing room. A wave of melancholy engulfed her. She remembered how Sam used to sit outside the dressing room holding her purse, grousing about how long it took her to try on clothes. She straightened her shoulders and said to herself, *Margaret, Sam is gone. He understands you need a new life. Now get a grip on yourself and let's see if these bathing suits are suitable bait for Mr. Next.*

Just as Margaret had donned her first suit, a voice shrieked out from the next dressing room stall.

"Oh my gawd!"

"Oh, Shirley, come out and let's see. It can't be that bad," she said.

"Oh, yes it is. Margaret, I don't know why you and Dorothy talked me into going bathing suit shopping."

"Hey, Shirley, it wasn't me," said Dorothy from the third stall. "You mentioned the sale at Dillards."

"And it was you who talked me into it," said Margaret.

"Well, just shoot me next time I say something so stupid. Who do they make bathing suits for these days? 14-year olds with anorexia?"

"You didn't actually try on the bikini, Shirley!"

"Margaret, I used to look great in a bikini."

"Yeah, in 1970. What is it with these suits? I've got on a nice little number with a flirty skirt but it only looks flirty on the hanger. I look like my mother in 1955. And even after all the aerobics classes, I've got these *bulges*."

"I'd give anything for a curve. I'm so skinny I look like a boy -- well an old platinum blonde boy."

"Don't complain, Dorothy. You can wear all the stuff that looks great on the models. Shirley and I look like models for the latest salami casings when we try that stuff on."

Margaret went on, mischievously, "Okay, I dare you both. We'll each put on another suit and come out to the three-way mirror. It will be good for a laugh."

Ten minutes later the three women, none of whom would ever see 60 again, stood in front of the triple mirror and laughed like teenagers until tears streamed down their faces.

Shirley, with her round face and a round figure, was testing the stretching limits of the spandex in a pink and purple one-piece suit with ruffles around the v-neckline. She kept tugging at the bottom of the suit which kept riding up to expose dimpled expanses of her broad rear end.

White-haired – she called it platinum blonde – Dorothy showed pale stick-thin arms and legs jutting out from a white and yellow polka-dotted two-piece suit. Her top was as flat as her stomach beneath, and the little skirt hovering above her thin legs looked like a lamp shade on a tall lamp.

A Clairol brunette, Margaret pretty well camouflaged her slightly pudgy figure in a blue and green two-piece suit with a long camisole top over boy-shorts, but whenever she moved, her bulgy mid-section made the material hanging below the bra ride up and exposed her rounded stomach making her look pregnant.

"I don't know about you," said Dorothy gasping for air after her laughing jag, "but I think I'll make my bathing suits do for another year or two until the designers' butts fall and boobs sag and girths grow and they start making suits for real people."

"I'm with you on that," said Shirley. "Let's go have one of those whip-creamy Starbucks and forget bathing suit shopping."

The three of them, again dressed in their slacks, shirts and athletic shoes, left the dressing room and headed to the center of the mall. A few minutes later, each had a frappuccino in front of her.

Margaret said, "I gave the last of Sam's clothes to the men's shelter this morning."

"I can't believe it took you so long. Sam's been gone for what, two years?"

"Two years and three months. It was really hard, Shirley. For the first few months I slept in a shirt I pulled out of the laundry basket after I got back from the hospital. It still smelled like him.

"And whenever I started to pack up his clothes to give away, I kept remembering what we did when he was wearing a sport coat or jacket or his tuxedo – going out New Year's Eve, dancing on a cruise, going out to the country club for dinner. Somehow, keeping them kept him close to me."

"Don't you fret over it." Dorothy patted the top of Margaret's hand. "Everyone handles grief differently. You just took a little longer to let go."

"Well, I finally have let go. And now I'm going to get out, find another man, and everything will be all right."

Dorothy and Shirley looked at each other, eyebrows raised.

"And how are you going to find this man?" asked Shirley.

"Well, I thought maybe you two might know someone."

"And just what are we looking for, my dear?" said Dorothy. "Someone who's tall, not overweight, good smile, hair on his head that isn't a toupee, financially well-set, with season tickets to the Ruth Eckerd Hall Broadway series? Oh yes, and he likes to cook and enjoys old movies and walks on the beach in the moonlight. Will that do it?"

Before Margaret could answer Shirley chimed in, "A little more definition here. Not just tall -- he has to be at least six feet tall. And he has to know how to dress. You know, doesn't wear plaids and stripes together and black socks with sneakers. And his teeth have to be his own – and not because he bought them! And he has to be healthy. Don't want to find yourself caring for an invalid. Let's see. He has to like the same kind of music you do. And not smoke – or chew tobacco. Absolutely has to love to dance.

"I think that's it. How does that sound, Margaret?"

"That would be perfect. Know someone like that?"

"Honey if I did, I'd think about trading in Fred for him," gleefully shrieked Dorothy.

"Hey, not if I saw him first," said Shirley.

"Well, it was worth asking. They say if you want to meet men, see if your friends will introduce you."

Dorothy leaned over and said, "News flash, Hon. That may work for people in their 20's and 30's, but when you get to the north side of 60 and beyond, the number of men still around is pretty thin, and any single woman who finds a halfway decent guy is going to keep him for herself. And I know a few married women who are keeping their eyes open just in case their worn-out spouses kick the bucket and they need replacements."

"Well, what am I going to do?" asked Margaret.

"Have you tried the classifieds?"

"Shirley, that's the first thing I did. And you know what? I can't find any. I tried the *St. Pete Times* and *Creative Loafing*. They both used to have personals. Not any more."

"You have to get modern, Margaret," said Shirley. "Use the internet. And have you seen those ads on TV for eHarmony.com?"

"Oh, I hate that smarmy-mouthed announcer."

"Yes, so do I. But it might work. And it's not the only match-making service around. Try the AARP web site. Maybe they've got one for old farts trying to find new wives."

"What about Publix?"

"What do you mean, Dorothy? Publix?"

"Honey, where have you been? Publix is *the* pick-up spot, especially for older folks. If you see a guy wandering around from aisle to aisle carrying a bag of cat food, he might not even have a cat. He's just waiting for a cat-lover to strike up a conversation. Or a guy might be standing over the meats, just waiting for the right woman to come along to answer his question about the best cuts to buy or how to cook them."

"Gee. Who knew? That sounds better than internet dating."

"Yeah, and you get to see what they really look like right off the bat."

"Thanks, Dorothy. I think I'll try Publix before I get into the computer world."

"Margaret," Shirley's face was serious and her eyes bored into Margaret's eyes. "Are you sure you want to find another husband?"

Margaret was taken aback. For a few moments her eyes focused downward at her half-drained cup of frappuccino as if it were the most fascinating thing she'd ever seen. Then she looked directly at Shirley and Dorothy. "Yes. I have to do this. I've been alone long enough. My life has to go on. Once I find another man, everything will be all right."

Shirley gave a "what can you do" shrug. "Okay."

The conversation went on to the water aerobics classes at the club house, the out-to-lunch bunch, who is this Justin Bieber anyway, and other mundane and lighthearted topics.

* * * * *

Margaret parked her Camry in the lot at the local Publix store. "Well, here goes nothing," she said as she got out of the car, straightened her shoulders and purposefully strode toward the entrance. "I still can't believe this is a place to meet men."

How silly to take so much trouble to dress for a trip to the super market. She wondered if the dangly blue earrings were too much. Her confidence gave way to self-consciousness as she pushed a cart slowly up an aisle furtively sizing up the men.

Publix seltzer was on sale. Of course, the large plastic bottles were on the top shelf and, with the front rank emptied out, Margaret couldn't reach them. She eyed the other people in the aisle and boldly approached a nice-looking, gray-haired man she judged to be a little older than herself.

"Excuse me, sir. Would you help me? I can't reach the seltzer and you're much taller than me."

"Sure, glad to help." He had a warm, deep voice. "How many do you want?"

"Two, thanks." *Got to talk a little more*, she thought. *Strike up a conversation before he walks away.* "Don't know if you use seltzer, but they're on sale – two 2-liter bottles for a dollar."

"Thanks. Didn't know that." He looked back over his shoulder and with a slightly raised voice said, "Hey, Michael. How are we fixed for seltzer?"

"Um. I'm not sure. I think we're fine, but it wouldn't hurt to buy a few. Just in case." He was younger, perfectly groomed, and spoke in the intimate way spouses do.

Margaret looked at Michael and at the gentleman who reached down the seltzer for her. *Oh.* Something clicked. She thanked the fellow again and pushed her cart down the aisle, trying not to giggle at the irony of it. *Here she was trying to pick up a man and the first one she approached was gay. Maybe this was the wrong Publix.*

Oh, well. Gotta eat so gotta shop. She headed toward the meat counters.

She held a package of chicken breasts when a skinny fellow with long sideburns framing his hang-dog face said, "Miss. How are you going to cook those?"

"Well, I haven't decided yet."

"I like chicken, but don't like them cooked with bones in. And the boneless ones are too expensive."

"Well, it's not too difficult to take the meat off the chicken bones. I do that a lot. Makes a more elegant chicken dish. You can even pound the chicken flat and . . ."

"Jared!" The shrill call came from behind the lanky guy, out of the pursed lips of a short and very round woman. Her tightly curled blond hair covered her head like a swimming cap. "Has he been bothering you?"

Without waiting for an answer, she said, "Will you stop annoying people!"

"I was just about to learn how you can take the bones off them chicken breasts."

"Dammit, Jared. Stop trying to tell me how to cook. The bones in them chickens don't hurt you. And I don't see you trying to cook them."

"Well, that's women's work. I was only trying . . . "

"You just shut up. Here's some men's work for you. Push this shopping cart to the check-out." She turned to Margaret. "Watch out for him if you see him again. He's just a trouble maker," and she waddled off behind her husband.

Well, I'm two for two so far, thought Margaret. *First a gay man and then a married guy. Wonder if anyone's found love among the lettuce here. Lettuce? Hmm, I need salad stuff.*

There were a few couples poking around the produce department. Margaret decided to abandon her manhunt for now, buy what she needed, and go home. This project was putting a strain on her.

She looked at the red leaf lettuce, disappointed at the small slightly withered heads. "Miss?" Margaret sought the source and faced a man who obviously worked there.

"Yes?"

"These are going to be removed. They're too old to sell. I'm just about to bring out some fresh heads. If you wait a few minutes, you'll have a better selection to choose from."

"Thanks. I appreciate that," she said. *Nice to know Publix service is still good. Even if they aren't so hot as matchmaking locales.*

"Back in a sec. Nice earrings," he said.

Well, she said to herself, *I don't remember the help here getting so personal!*

* * * * *

The rhythmic beat of the music from the next aerobics class throbbed in the background as Shirley and Margaret headed for the locker room.

"I can't believe it!" said Shirley, wiping her forehead and flushed face with her towel.

"I couldn't make up what happened in Publix if I tried," replied Margaret, panting. "Whew. These aerobics classes better be doing me some good. I'm exhausted."

"You hit on a gay man and a married guy hit on you?"

"Well, I didn't exactly 'hit' on the gay. And I did need the seltzer."

"Yeah, but . . ."

Dorothy came over and interrupted. "Well, do we get to be bridesmaids yet? Did you meet Mr. Right in the pet food aisle?"

"Yes, I met Mr. Right," Margaret snapped. "But not in the pet food aisle last week. I met him at church almost 40 years ago. And I married him. And he died.

"I'm just looking for, um, Mr. Next. And Publix absolutely did not work for me as a place to meet men. Shirley can tell you the whole story later."

"Well, SORRY for being inquisitive," Dorothy was clearly miffed. "Just thought if Publix didn't work out, you'd like to know that the country club is having a singles night next Tuesday. You don't belong, but Shirley does. Why don't you both go? Maybe you two singles will get lucky."

"Awww, Dorothy, I'm not into that. I like my life as it is. With aerobics and Mahjong and bingo and canasta and walking Wilbur and being on the homeowners association, I don't have any time for a man."

"Oh, Shirley, just go and be a wallflower. Take Margaret so she can meet some men."

"I don't want to put you out, Shirley. You don't have to go on my account."

"No, Margaret, Dorothy's right. Besides, there's nothing good on the TV on Tuesday night anyway. Might as well."

* * * * *

Tuesday evening Shirley ushered Margaret into the casual bar area of the country club. A bartender was at the ready at the shiny oak bar; a banquet table opposite the bar held a few platters of cheese and crackers and grapes; in between was a collection of middle and late-aged men and women in a range of shapes and sizes.

"I feel so self-conscious. Everyone's going to know I'm looking for a man."

"Margaret, what do you think everyone else is doing here? These guys didn't come so they could talk golf together. I bet even the bartender is single and looking."

"I don't think it would work between me and a bartender. They work evenings."

"That was a joke. Looks like there's quite a few men here to pick from. Go find yourself a man. I'm going to find a margarita and a nice comfortable chair in a corner."

A few moments after Shirley left her, Margaret felt a light tap on her shoulder.

"Hello, Miss. Are you here for the singles Meet and Mingle?" He was a slender, pleasant looking man except for his thick glasses and tufts of gray hair sprouting out of his ears.

"Yes, I am. My name is Margaret."

"Pleased to meet you. I'm George. Are you a healthy person?"

Margaret was taken aback. "Um. Yes, I guess so. Why do you ask?"

"Well, I don't want to waste my time on someone who's got cancer or some other serious illness. I don't want to be a nursemaid to a dying woman. I want someone healthy who'll take care of me in my old age. Been having some problems. Old ticker isn't what it used to be, you know. Looks like you'll do."

"Th-th-thank you for the assessment," stammered Margaret. "But, if you'll excuse me, I have to check on my friend." She searched for Shirley and located her sitting back in a corner laughing with a chubby, bald-headed man standing by her chair. *Oh, darn. Shirley probably doesn't want me interrupting, but I have to get away from this jerk.*

"Just checking in with you. I had to escape someone who was interviewing me to be a nurse for his old age!"

"Oh, my. I guess it takes all kinds. This is Cyrus. He's a real hoot," said Shirley. "Cy just came because his friend Fred was afraid to come alone. Cyrus, this is my friend Margaret." He shook her hand and gave her a nice how-do-you-do. "Now you go try again. All these men can't be nincompoops!"

* * * * *

"Dorothy, it was absolutely incredible." Margaret and Shirley had cups of coffee in front of them as they sat at a round glass-topped table on Dorothy's lanai.

"Margaret, I'd believe anything these days. Here," she thrust forward a plate laden with small pastries, "have something to eat and tell me about last night."

"Well, the first man I met wanted to make sure I was healthy because he had a bad heart and wanted someone to nurse him in his old age.

"Then I met a tall, handsome man who was a great conversationalist. He was widely traveled and hoped to meet a woman who would like to see more of the world with him. But all the time he talked to me he kept farting. Loudly. And they were ugly stinky farts. He didn't seem to even notice or mind that we were in a cloud of swamp gas."

Shirley and Dorothy doubled up in laughter. Margaret broke down laughing, too.

"And then there was the fat drunk. He was in a barber shop quartet. He almost strangled me with his arm around my neck trying to get me to sing 'Sweet Adeline' with him."

"Come on, Margaret. There must have been some normal human males there."

"I did meet two fellows who seemed pretty okay, or at least normal compared to the others. One was Harold, a retired accountant. He looked okay, but all he talked about was tax write-offs and depreciation and accounting stuff. He didn't seem to have any other interests. The last book he read was about international banking and money laundering.

"The other one was Al. I don't know what he did for a living. He talked mostly about how he misses his late wife and how nice it was to have companionship – and his golf game. I told him about Sam's passing."

"And?" Dorothy leaned over the table expectantly. "Did you make a date with either of them?"

"No. We did exchange telephone numbers. And both of them suggested getting together for coffee or dinner sometime."

"Well, that's progress. Never know what might come of it."

"I think Shirley found the only fun guy there."

"What?" Dorothy's mouth gaped as if she'd seen an orange elephant pass by on roller skates. "I thought . . ."

"Yes, I know. And I wasn't going there to meet men. I told you. My life is busy enough without complicating it by throwing a man into the mix.

"Cyrus saw me sitting alone in the corner and struck up a conversation. He wasn't there to meet women. Only came to the singles thing because his friend didn't want to go alone. We got to talking and had a good time. That's all there is to it."

"Shirley, are you telling me he didn't get your phone number?"

"Yes, Margaret, I gave him my number," Shirley gave her a sharp, one-eyebrow-raised look. "But that doesn't mean he's going to call or we're going out together!"

"Wouldn't you know it? I'm trying to find a man and the woman who is just along for the company comes up with a winner. Somebody up there doesn't like me!" Margaret pointed to the ceiling. "Maybe it's time to give the internet a try. So how do I start?"

"Hey, I'm married and Fred wouldn't like me trolling for another man. I haven't got a clue about internet dating except for the ads I see on TV," said Dorothy.

"Me, either," said Shirley. "I know. Talk to Mabel."

"Mabel?"

"Yeah. She doesn't let it get around, but she's been internet dating for the past few years."

"I guess it doesn't work if she hasn't found the right guy in all that time."

"You never know, Margaret," said Shirley. "Get some advice from Mabel and give it a try. What do you have to lose?"

* * * * *

Margaret sat on a blue, white and orange tropical print chair in Mabel's living room, a glass of iced tea on the coffee table between her and her hostess.

"All right, dear," Margaret leaned forward expectantly as Mabel continued, "here's the deal. There are some free internet dating services out there. But I figure, is that the kind of man you want to meet, a guy who's either too cheap to pay something to meet the right woman, or, worse, too broke to afford it?"

Mabel was talking so authoritatively, Margaret felt she should be taking notes.

"How much does it cost to do one of the pay sites?"

"Not much: e-Harmony charges about $30 a month. And you can quit any time. Of course, you can go into it big-time and find some on-line services and even personal match-makers that cost hundreds or even a few thousand dollars. But I doubt you get any more for your money."

"How does it work?"

"First you describe yourself, you know, some kind of mini-biography and a picture, and you describe what you want in a man. You know, non-smoker, born-again Christian, in good physical shape, plays tennis, hula hoop champion, likes classic movies. Anything you think would help match up you and a guy.

"And you might as well ignore the 'desired body shape' the guys put down. I never, ever saw one who said he'd like someone a little pudgy or someone who wears a size 18 or larger. They all want slender. I'll give them slender – in their dreams. They sit there with their pot bellies and jowly faces and want Miss America. Hah." Mabel had a definite paunch, but her bright blue eyes and violently red spiked hair were what you noticed first.

"Well, what happens next?"

"You look on the web site at the guys who are close to matching what you said you wanted in a man. If any of them look good, you can e-mail them. And about that looking good: some of them look great in their pictures, then you meet them and find out that the picture was taken some years ago, like when they had hair!

"Anyway, if you e-mail a bit and then want to talk, you can exchange phone numbers. And if that seems to work, you can meet in person."

"Wow. Seems like a lot of work. And a lot to be wary of."

"Well, my dear, you can just go down to the nearest Irish-style pub and randomly pick up someone sitting at the bar alone drinking a beer. All you know about him is that he drinks beer and is alone."

"I guess you're right. At least you know something about the guys you meet on-line."

"You've got that right, Margaret. And if you don't have a good feeling about them when you start e-mailing, you don't have to worry about how to dump them. You just say he doesn't seem to be your type and go on to the next one."

"Okay. I'll try it."

* * * * *

Margaret got a cup of coffee at the coffee bar and sat at a table near the window where she could easily see all the customers coming through the door. A handsome man with dark hair and piercing blue eyes entered and scanned the room. *Wow,* she wondered, *why would he need an on-line dating service? Could he be the one?* He looked to be on the youngish side of 60, but maybe he was just, as they said, very well preserved. *Pictures on the internet don't necessarily look like the person. Maybe this is Hugh.* She was about to wave when his face broke out in a movie-star smile and he strode toward a beautiful young blonde seated at a table toward the rear.

Oh, well. I can only dream. Sam was nice looking, but no movie star. It's what's inside that counts. But it might be nice. . .

The door swung open and gave forth a mountain of a man, neatly bearded, wiping his brow with a large red checkered handkerchief. Margaret judged him to be at least 6'3" and maybe 40 pounds overweight. *No wonder he's sweating*, thought Margaret. *It's 80 degrees outside and he's wearing a tweed sport coat. Probably thinks it makes him look like a professor. It really makes him look like he hasn't got the sense God gave a turtle. Fortunately he doesn't look like the picture of Hugh I saw on-line.*

The man scanned around the room, obviously searching for someone. Margaret had a sinking feeling. *Was Mr. Senseless her coffee date?* He saw her and came over.

"Margaret?"

"Yes."

"Hi, I'm Hugh, Hugh Rainier, like Prince Rainier of Monaco. No relation, unfortunately." He shoved the hankie in his pocket and offered her a beefy hand. She offered her hand, fearing crushed bones, but was grateful for a firm, quick grasp.

"I wouldn't have recognized you from your picture."

"Sorry about that. Grew the beard a few years ago when I was hired to teach English lit at St. Petersburg College. I was trying to look a little more professorial."

Aha! I was right!

"And I'm a little sensitive about the few pounds I've put on since then. Don't like having my picture taken to remind me of it."

A few pounds? A few more than a few, thought Margaret. Hugh's on-line photo made him look slightly underweight.

"Is that coffee you're drinking? May I get you another when I get mine? Or would you like something to eat?"

"No, but thanks."

Hugh returned with a coffee and a brownie. Margaret understood his weight issue. He looked down at his brownie, then at her and said, "That's my problem: I'm a very oral person. I like to eat. Could be worse. I could have a drinking problem instead."

Barely taking a breath, he went on, "You sounded like a lovely person on the phone, Margaret. And you look just like your picture, quite pretty in a mature way." Margaret wasn't sure how to take that, but she accepted it as a compliment.

"Thank you."

"No need to thank me for telling the truth! I wasn't brought up to lie. You know it's tough to meet attractive women who are in your own generation. As an adjunct professor I have a lot of women in my classes. Some of them are drawn to me as an authority figure or as someone with status. And some even hit on me. But, really, I'm 60 years old."

Margaret was skeptical. His biography said "60's," and she pegged him at a few years older than what he was claiming.

"What do I have in common with a 24 or 25 or even 30 year old? I want someone who knows about Viet Nam and landing a man on the moon and Ronald Reagan's presidency from having been there, not from a history book. Unfortunately, some young women these days aren't even familiar with these events from books. What happened to a good liberal education? And although I try to keep up with the times, I do like songs that have recognizable tunes and lyrics, and lyrics I wouldn't be ashamed to have my mother hear.

"And that's what's nice about these internet dating sites. Without them, we wouldn't be here enjoying a pleasant conversation.

"We talked on the phone about opera. Have you been to any local productions? I find the ones at Ruth Eckerd Hall to be acceptable, but they don't hold a candle to the Sarasota Opera productions. They're so richly staged that the same music and the same story seem so different. I haven't made it over to see any opera in Tampa, even though it's closer than Sarasota.

"So what is your favorite opera, besides *Carmen*, which everyone loves because it's got everything – familiar music, a love story, intrigue, violence." He paused and Margaret was surprised that she was actually going to get a chance to talk while he took a big bite of his brownie.

"*Tosca*. That's my favorite after *Carmen*. "

"Great opera. One of my favorites, too. Of course, it's the ultimate in tragic operas. Normally the hero or heroine dies at the end. But in *Tosca* everybody dies at the end, at least all the major characters. Of course, you knew that."

Margaret was pleased that as the conversation progressed, it actually turned into a dialogue instead of a monologue. They talked about their travels, both past and future, about restaurants in the local area and the state of today's movie industry. Margaret suspected that Hugh monopolized the conversation at first because he was as nervous as she at their meeting in person. By the time they parted an hour later, she had decided that he was a pleasant companion. They agreed to talk again soon.

* * * * *

"Rrrrrrring." Margaret picked up the phone halfway hoping it was Hugh at the other end. "Hello."

"Hi, Margaret. This is Al. We met at the country club a few weeks ago at the singles event. You told me about Sam and I told you about how I lost my Wendy."

"Oh, hi!"

"I just called to chat a bit. I'm not interrupting anything, am I?"

"No. I'm just having a quiet evening at home."

"I don't know if I told you that I'm a realtor. Had to do something to keep myself occupied. Not that this is the greatest way to keep occupied since the housing market went bust."

"I'm glad I don't have to sell my home now. Sam and I -- I mean, I own it free and clear. I feel sorry for people who can't afford their mortgages and are desperate to sell."

"You've got that right, Margaret. But you'd be sitting pretty even if you decided to sell. I used a reverse phone look-up and found where you live and did a little look at the market in your area."

Margaret felt angry heat rise in her cheeks. *How dare this casual acquaintance blatantly pry into the value of her home!*

Oblivious to his effect on her, Al continued, "You and your husband made a good choice when you bought in that neighborhood. When homes are listed there – at least when they're listed at realistic prices – they sell pretty quickly, some in a week or two, and most within 60 days. It's the location, the neighborhood, and how people keep up their property. You know, if you ever think of selling, I'd be happy to do a market analysis for you and do the listing."

Margaret struggled to control her resentment at his personal intrusion and said, curtly, "Furthest thing from my mind."

"Well, I have a lot of good contacts and can get you some good prices if you want to remodel or update."

"Nice of you to offer."

Al continued on and Margaret envisioned thirty minutes of boring real estate war stories and gossip. He'd already rubbed her the wrong way, so Margaret tried to disengage.

"Gee, Al. Nice talking with you, but it's getting late and I have some housework I was going to finish tonight." *Being pleasant doesn't cost anything*, she thought.

"Oh, sorry. Here I am running on. It's just nice to talk with a pretty, intelligent woman who hasn't got me running all over town to try to find her a house.

"Say, maybe we could get together sometime. Maybe go out for a bite. Or, how's this? Sometimes there are open houses at some of the top of the line, most expensive homes in the area for real estate agents only. These mansions are really something. Maybe if one comes up in the next week or so, you can come along with me to look at it. I'll take you along as my associate."

"That sounds interesting." And it did sound interesting to her. It was just unfortunate that it came along with Al's company.

"Great. I'll call you if an opportunity pops up. And, in any case, I'll call and we can go out. Maybe to Tarpon Springs for some Greek food."

"All right. Talk with you later. Bye for now." *All right? Oh, why did I say that? He's a bore. And he has an oily personality, the kind that makes me want to count my fingers if I shake hands with him. Oh, well. I can always say no if he calls for a date.*

She hung up the phone and sat down with her book. Ten minutes later the phone rang again. *Was it Hugh?*

"Hello."

"Hi, Margaret. This is Harold. We met at the country club singles evening a few weeks ago. Do you remember me? I'm a retired accountant."

"Yes, I do remember you, Harold. How are you?"

"Oh, pretty good. Enjoying my off-season. See, I volunteer to be an AARP tax preparer from January to April. Have to take training in December. And then additional training when Congress passes a last minute tax change. You know they've done that a lot in the last few years."

"Oh, that's interesting." *It wasn't really.* "What do you do in your off-season?"

"I'm a financial advisor. I help people make sure they've got their money where it's doing the best for them. I'm especially busy right from March to July, after my clients file their tax returns and decide they're paying too much in taxes.

"Say, if you ever want any investment advice, I'd be happy to give you a free analysis and make some recommendations," he sounded so positive and chipper Margaret thought he was going to throw in a free toaster if she took him up on his offer.

"Gee, thanks. But my nephew is a financial planner and he's helping me manage my money."

"I understand. That's great. But in case you want a second opinion – heh, heh, sounds like we're doctors, doesn't it – I'd be happy to help out." *Maybe a waffle iron instead of a toaster.*

"Do you do anything that isn't financial?"

"I canoe. I take my little canoe all over the middle part of Florida on rivers and lakes. I see lots of fish and other critters – otters, possums, armadillos and, of course, gators. I give the gators a wide berth.

"Have you ever canoed?"

"Not since I went to a kids' camp in central Wisconsin. Aren't canoes dangerous?"

"Only if you try to stand up in them. It's kind of peaceful to glide along in a canoe. Not like in motor boats that scare all the wildlife away before you get to see them.

"Do you think you'd like to go out with me in my canoe sometime?"

"That might be fun."

"I try to get out about once a month. My schedule is pretty busy and that's all I can break away. I'll call you next time I plan a day on the water."

"Okay, but nothing too strenuous for my first time paddling a canoe in fifty years."

"Say, would you like to have coffee tomorrow afternoon? I have a late morning appointment and another at three p.m. But we could meet at one o'clock at Tiffany's Restaurant. Know where it is? On U.S. 19 just south of Alderman."

Should I? Or is this going to be a waste of time? Oh, well, nothing ventured, nothing gained. "Sure, I know where Tiffany's is. I'll meet you there tomorrow at one."

She hung up the phone and wondered if she was losing her mind getting into this dating thing. She read a little, glancing over at the phone, trying to will Hugh to call. Finally, she gave up on the evening and went to bed.

* * * * *

Margaret and Dorothy pushed their carts past the meat counters in Publix. Margaret quickly eyed the other customers, to make sure that Jared, who'd accosted her by the chicken breasts, was nowhere in sight.

"My goodness, woman, you're the belle of the ball," said Dorothy as she threw a pack of pork chops into her basket and turned toward the produce section.

"Having a few phone calls and coffee dates hardly makes me Scarlett O'Hara," responded Margaret. "And I've only had one coffee date with Hugh. The other one with Harold is this afternoon."

"Well, if your dance card isn't full, you still have to keep your eyes open here at Publix. Why, I had a guy hit on me last week in the cereal aisle."

"No! What was wrong with him?"

"Margaret! You insult me to assume that only someone undesirable would hit on me." Dorothy raised her head in mock disdain.

"Actually, I have to admit that even if I didn't have dear old Fred at home, I wouldn't have been interested in a bald little runt with coke-bottle glasses and bad breath." She and Margaret laughed at that.

"Hello, miss." It was the produce man who'd gotten her the nice red leaf lettuce a few weeks back.

"Hello."

"I thought you might like to know that we just got in some nice new Boston lettuce. People who think iceberg is real lettuce don't appreciate it, but someone like you who buys red and green leaf lettuce probably recognizes how good it is. And it's a nice buy at $1.69 a package."

"Thank you. Where is it?"

"Right over there next to the bunches of parsley. And if you ever need anything special in produce, just ask for Warren. That's me. I'd be happy to help you."

"Thank you, Warren," said Margaret. *The people who work at Publix are always so helpful,* she thought.

"I'm anxious to hear how your coffee date goes this afternoon. Fred's got us going on a bus to the Hard Rock Casino in a few hours and we won't be home until late. I'll catch up with you tomorrow."

"If you can't get a hold of me tomorrow, try Shirley. She's coming over after supper and I'll tell her all about it.

"Would you believe she wants to learn how to knit so she can make a cap to cover dear Cyrus's bald head in the wintertime?"

"Oh my God. Shirley getting all domestic? What's this Cyrus got?"

"Right now it looks like he's got Shirley." They laughed and parted ways.

* * * * *

Shirley gushed out questions before she even sat down in Margaret's living room that evening.

"All right, Margaret. Before we get to this knitting thing, tell me what happened with your coffee date this afternoon. Was it fun? What's Harold like?"

"A cheap snake."

"What?"

"A cheap snake. We met for coffee at Tiffany's. But when he got there he said he hadn't had time to grab lunch, so he ordered coffee and a burger.

"We had a nice conversation. He brought a map showing me the locations of his favorite canoeing spots. Suggested that he'd provide the canoe and the transportation and maybe I'd pack a picnic lunch for the two of us. That seemed reasonable."

"Sounds good, so far."

"Well it got bad, Shirley. When the waitress brought the bill, I said I'd pay for my own coffee. Harold said no and insisted that he pay. After all, he invited me. And then he searches in all his pockets and says he forgot his wallet."

"No. You're kidding. He's a financial planner and a tax preparer? And he conveniently forgot his wallet?" Shirley's eyes widened in disbelief.

"Right. I ended up paying for his lunch."

"Of course, he promised to pay you back, didn't he?"

"Sure he did. But he didn't ask where he could send a check or set a time when we could meet to give me the money or make any move toward arranging how to reimburse me.

"Then I suggested he should drive very carefully if he was on the road without his driver's license. And he flipped open a flat little case that had just his drivers license and auto registration – said he always had that with him. But I thought I saw the edge of a credit card or two in there, too."

"He could have paid with his credit card but he stuck you with the bill instead? You're right. What a cheap snake. Write him off."

"Don't worry, Shirley. I already did."

"Okay, now about this knitting stuff, Margaret."

The phone rang before Margaret could start her handiwork tutoring session. She smiled and said, "I hope that's Hugh. So far he's the best of the bunch."

Shirley looked on as her friend picked up the phone and smiled..

"Hello . . . Yes, this is Margaret . . . Nice to hear from you, too, Hugh . . . Eeek!" Margaret dropped the phone on the floor as if it had burned her hand.

"What's wrong, Margaret? Are you okay?" Shirley leapt up from the sofa and rushed over to her friend. "What should I do?"

"Hang it up! Hang it up!" She cringed away from the phone.

"Well, what was that all about? Was it Hugh? Or an obscene phone call."

"Yes."

"Well?"

"He told me he would like to spread guacamole all over my body and then proceed to lick it all off."

Shirley's jaw dropped. Then she got a gleam in her eye and said, "So are you going to take him up on it?"

The two women burst out in hysterical laughter and eventually got around to the knitting lesson.

* * * * *

"It's a good thing I take these aerobics classes for myself and not for some guy," said Margaret, bending over and breathing heavily.

"I've got to admit, none of the guys you've met so far seem worth the effort."

Margaret straightened up and stood with her hands on her hips facing Shirley. "Wish I had your luck. Cyrus seems to be such a nice guy."

"Yeah, he is. And he's not pushy. You know, you meet a guy and all of a sudden he wants to be in your face all the time. Not with Cyrus. He golfs and belongs to some clubs and has grandchildren in the area, so we get together maybe once or twice a week and have some fun. And that's enough."

"I keep hoping I'll find someone like that. Then everything will be all right."

"Margaret! What's wrong, honey?" Shirley grabbed for her friend as she paled, gasped for air and collapsed to the floor.

* * * * *

"Don't scare us like that, Margaret!" Dorothy came cruising into the hospital room with Shirley in tow.

"Hey, I didn't faint deliberately. It just happened. And now I get a Medicare-paid night in this fancy hospital bed at Mease Countryside Hospital. For nothing."

"Fainting like that isn't exactly nothing," said Shirley. "You scared me half to death when you collapsed like that."

"Wonder what happened?" asked Dorothy. "When I called, you said all the tests came back all right and they couldn't find anything wrong with you. No updates on that?"

"Nope. Dorothy, I'm a medical mystery."

"Well, that's good. As far as I can tell, the only thing wrong with you is the way you pick men!"

"Oh, don't rub it in. I assume Shirley told you about my phone call from Hugh."

"Sure did. I was going to bring you some guacamole in case you wanted to practice with an intern."

"That's not even funny. He said he was an oral person. But I had no idea!"

The three chatted a while and Margaret's two visitors promised to pick her up when she was released the next morning.

A few minutes after Shirley and Dorothy left, a young woman delivered a tray with the dinner Margaret had ordered from the hospital menu. She was pleasantly surprised. The salad looked fresh and under the warming domes the salmon, rice and vegetables were nicely arranged. She soon confirmed that everything tasted as good as it looked. *Nice to have a good meal that I didn't have to cook,* she thought. *I guess I can handle being in the hospital one night.*

She read a bit after dinner and decided that she might as well try to sleep. It would help her pass the time. She was irritated that she couldn't be released until morning, even though the tests all came back showing that there was nothing wrong with her. *After all, what's a little fainting spell.*

Margaret tossed and turned, unable to sleep with the din around her. *Why are hospitals so noisy? Don't they know there are sick people here? And why does the staff think they have to yell at each other down the hall?*

Resigned, she tried counting backwards from 100. Sometimes that worked when she had infrequent bouts of insomnia. About to drop off, she heard women's voices outside her door and she was awake again. Margaret speculated, *Maybe if I swear at them, they'll shut up – or at least move somewhere else.* Then she overheard what they were saying.

"I'm so sorry about Aunt Pat. I'm glad we could be here for her at the end."

"Yes, me, too. What's saddest is that she refused to have the life she wanted so badly."

"You're right. I know Kit will be happy to get her prized Limoges china and the silver service for twelve. Aunt Pat took them out and showed them to me sometimes. But, you know, I don't think she ever used them. She was always saving them for some special event that never came. The same with the good table linens. I think Marcy is supposed to get those. Too bad she never had children she could pass them on to. I guess she never got around to that either."

"Yes, that was Aunt Pat. She put everything off until later. I've heard for years about the trip she planned to New York so she could attend the theater every night and throw in a matinee on Saturday."

"And her cruise down the Nile! That was going to be the highlight of her travels, of all the travels that never happened. We heard for years about what she was going to do someday. And now she's dead. She never got to 'someday.'"

Margaret heard the choke in their voices and imagined from the sounds that the two women outside her door were now hugging each other and crying.

And Margaret felt tears flow down her cheeks. *That poor woman. She didn't know how to live. She was probably afraid to try to turn her plans into real life experiences.*

Suddenly, Margaret saw clearly into her own life. *What am I doing? Am I looking for a husband so I don't have to think about what to do with my life?* She used the edge of the sheet to wipe away her tears. It was time to give herself a good talking to. *Margaret, don't be an idiot. Don't end up like Aunt Pat. Live the life you want. You don't need a man to do that. Florida is wonderful. It has beaches and nature preserves and cruise ships that sail from its ports and airlines with good connections to everywhere in the world. All you have to do is forget about finding a man and everything will be all right.*

And she started to cry again, this time tears of relief.

* * * * *

Dorothy and Shirley showed up at nine the next morning. As they entered Margaret's room she greeted them with, "Get me out of here! I have places to go and things to do!"

She was dressed, sitting in the chair in her room, with a plastic bag labeled "patient belongings" by her side. "The nurse says I have to have someone here when I sign the release papers. Would you believe it? And they won't let me walk down to the car. I have to be taken down in a wheelchair."

"Okay. Ring for the nurse and let's get on the road," said Shirley.

"What's all this excitement about places to go and things to do?" asked Dorothy. "Don't tell me you've managed to meet a doctor who's interested in you."

"No. It's not that at all. I just don't want to turn into an Aunt Pat. Oh, here's the nurse. I'll tell you later."

As Dorothy drove them away from the hospital, Margaret shared her revelation about how she was wasting her life looking for a man and the sad story of Aunt Pat that caused this insight.

"Wow," said Shirley. "That's quite an about face for you. You spend time looking for a man. I find Cyrus. And you find out that you want your own life, not a man. Strange are the ways of the world, indeed."

Dorothy said, "Well, on to practical matters. I have to stop at Publix for a few things. Anyone mind?"

"No, I need a few things," said Shirley.

"Me too," added Margaret.

A few minutes later Margaret was in the produce section, looking for fresh parsley.

"Hi. It's nice to see you here again," said a pleasant voice.

Margaret looked up, "Hi, Warren."

"I'm happy you remembered my name. Beats having someone call me boy when they want something, me, a 67-year-old man!"

"They don't do that? Do they?"

"You'd be surprised. Not everyone is as pleasant and courteous as you," said Warren. "I hope you won't think me too forward, but I never see you here with a man. And I'm a widower. Maybe we can be friends.

"I was wondering if you'd like to go out to lunch with me some day this week. And I have season tickets to the Broadway series at Ruth Eckerd Hall. If we get along, maybe you'd come with me sometime?"

His face reddened, "I'm sorry . . . I'm going too fast. Maybe we should start with lunch. Of course, I'd have to know your name to ask you properly."

She smiled and said, "My name is Margaret."

And she knew that no matter what happened, everything would be all right.

FANTASY BOUND

by

Arlene Trainor Corby

The calendar on the fridge door displayed a tropical scene. Andrea could almost feel the wind blowing through the palm trees. She imagined the salt smell coming off the waves spraying across the turquoise colored sea. On the horizon, a sailboat beckoned the viewer to climb aboard. In the foreground, light beige sand invited a bare foot to leave its print.

Andrea picked this calendar to keep her winter blues at bay. She hoped it would transmit, at least in thought, warmth and dream material to help pass the coming cold weather. Winter was not her favorite time of year. Inside her tiny apartment, the furnace had blasted non-stop since early October as uninvited frost formed on the window sill. It seemed that Philly was experiencing an exceptionally cold fall. Depressed, Andrea watched the brightly colored leaves fall listlessly to the ground. They didn't like the coming of winter either.

Rising early, she made her way to the kitchen table where the percolator brewed a strong cup of coffee. She and Sean, her boyfriend of two years, had planned this vacation as an escape from the winter blues and the stress of their jobs. She poured coffee into her mug and stared at the calendar. Penciled X's marked off the days before they would drive to Key West's renowned Halloween celebration called "Fantasy Fest." In Tuesday's box, red ink read "Fantasy Bound" and today was that day. Resting against the staircase was her orange backpack filled with summer clothes. Within an hour, it would be in the trunk of Sean's car and they would be on their way.

Friends related stories of the beauty of Bahia Honda State Park, which wasn't far from Key West. They suggested camping and advised early booking because the campground fills up quickly, especially around Key West holidays. Andrea did an internet search and found pictures of beautiful beaches, sunsets, all surrounded by tropical waters. It was easy to see why advanced bookings were necessary. Located on Big Pine Key, Bahia Honda State Park has the Gulf of Mexico on one side and the Atlantic Ocean on the other, just a thirty-five mile drive to Key West. Andrea and Sean agreed that camping would save them a lot of money.

On the table by the door lay all the paperwork needed for their escape: campground reservation, website print-outs, a road atlas, and a detailed map of downtown Key West. On top of that was the all-important iPhone with apps for GPS maps, weather predictions and cheap gas.

Sean arrived at eight o'clock with a to-go cup of coffee in hand. Showing off, he gallantly lifted Andrea's backpack with one hand while balancing the coffee in the other. Andrea laughed.

"Are you ready for the long trip ahead?" he teased. She felt excitement and happiness in her heart for his company and the upcoming trip. After several years of dating losers, she thought she would never find a decent, warm human being who would respect her for who she was. When she met Sean a few summers back, something clicked. He was comfortable to be around and very considerate of her needs.

"Glad to be going with you," she smiled and squeezed his arm.

Outside, he clicked his fob which opened the trunk, and stowed her backpack next to his. Nestled toward the back of the trunk were their tent and sleeping bags.

"Yes, it's going to be a long drive, so let's get going," Andrea joked.

"Are you ready for a fantasy?" asked Sean.

"Every time I'm with you, it's a fantasy," replied a blushing Andrea.

Bundled in down jackets, scarves, wool hats and gloves they set out for a week of fun in the sun. Andrea thought, just like the Jimmy Buffett lyric, "They're going where winter spends the summer."

Sean estimated it would take twenty-four hours. They planned to drive straight down Interstate 95, stopping only for necessities and quick naps. Additional company was sought from their MP3 players to set the beat for a jammin' island adventure and the warmth of the lower latitudes. A variety of island music would blast from their car speakers.

The Honda Accord buzzed down the highway. Jersey, Virginia, and the Carolinas zoomed by. Somewhere in Georgia the temperature started to rise as the compass pointed due south. Their plan of sharing the drive and taking naps worked well. All the while, the beat of drums kept up with the speed of the car or the car kept up with the beat of the drums.

On the way Andrea questioned Sean, "Do you think Fantasy Fest is going to be too much? I mean with all the crowds and drinking. I heard last year there were a few muggings and flaming gay guys who really flaunted their, uh, apparatus."

Sean replied, "It will be what it will be. That is what adventure is all about. Don't worry, we will be together and that is all that is important." Andrea had never done anything so risky. Part of her felt scared and part of her was ready for the excitement of the unknown.

The Overseas Highway started at Florida City, Mile Marker 127.5. However, the tropical feel of the Keys wouldn't start until Key Largo. That is when they would be surrounded by water. It would take about twenty two hours from the time they left Philly, to Flagler's Seven Mile Bridge, once just a railroad track, now a beautiful two lane highway.

Early Wednesday morning, a bright yellow sun rose in the east. Its rays illuminated the shimmering turquoise waters of the Atlantic. Andrea and Sean agreed to slow down. They got out of the car, inhaled the sea breezes, and took in the scenery. Most importantly, they wanted to feel the long awaited warmth of the sun. As a reality check, Sean reached for the iPhone which read 37 degrees in Philly with a wind chill of 20. The temperature in Key West read low 80s and sunny. Being aware of the sun's harmful rays, they slathered themselves with coconut suntan lotion. Its familiar smell reminded them of summer.

Andrea had known about Flagler's railroad and its importance to the development of Key West, but wanted to know more. Before they left, she went on line and downloaded a few facts that she thought Sean would like to know. Seeing the bridge laid out in front of them was the perfect moment for her to share her new found knowledge. Back in the car, she asked Sean, "Did you know that the railroad was completed in 1912? Construction began in 1905 with a labor force of over 4,000 men."

Sean quickly calculated the construction time. "That's over seven years to complete! Can you imagine the labor force needed for this project?"

Andrea continued, "It was originally called the *Florida East Coast Railroad* and the most treacherous part is under us right now. The building of the Seven Mile Bridge had been hampered by deep water and strong currents making working conditions very difficult. Once completed, Key West became a desirable destination for wealthy northerners to escape winter, and summer cottages sprang up for the wealthy. To accommodate this growth, the population swelled with people and services to support this new era."

Whether rich or poor, the economic depression didn't hold back the flow of tourists. Flagler opened up the tropics to thousands of vacationers.

"Listen to this," Andrea excitingly read on. "When the U.S. decided to build the Panama Canal, Flagler's vision foresaw ports in Key West that would transfer passengers, cars and cargo to his steamship line and ferry them to Havana. Their final destination would be the Panama Canal. There, goods would be transferred to go on to Latin America."

Sean wondered out loud, "If Flagler had been successful, how would our relations with Cuba be today?"

"Well," Andrea replied, "I guess the Cuban Missile Crisis wouldn't have happened, so who knows? Things would be very different."

Knowing that the Keys are prone to hurricanes, Sean asked, "Where there any hurricanes that affected the building of the railroad?"

"Definitely," replied Andrea. "The 1935 'Great Labor Day Hurricane' packed winds in excess of 200 miles an hour and obliterated 40 miles of track. It went down as the most powerful storm in record keeping history. Since the bridges and viaducts were built of concrete, they were undamaged. Seeing a way to open up the Keys to tourism, in 1977 Congress approved funds to build a new Overseas Highway, for cars only. Today, the two-lane highway spans seven miles of the straight and narrow, over azure blue waters."

Sean laughed as he commented, "The road may be straight and narrow, but I hope the path becomes bizarre and crazy once we get to Key West."

A billboard at Mile Marker 82 advertised a restaurant called The Islamorada Island Grill. It showed a long wharf inviting dinners to "drink and eat in a tropical setting." As if on cue, Sean's stomach made a growling sound.

"Did you hear that?" he questioned Andrea. "Let's eat."

The restaurant looked just like the billboard. Getting out of the car, they walked along the wharf that rose several feet above the water. Below swam schools of tarpon fish. "Hmmm," Sean quizzed, "I wonder if they're gonna wind up on the menu?" At the end of the wharf, a canvas awning shaded tables that invited guest to enjoy lunch.

"What do the locals like to eat?" Sean asked the waiter.

"Stone crabs and Key Lime pie," he replied.

Sean and Andrea didn't even read the menu and ordered what the waiter had suggested. When the stone crabs arrived, Sean was surprised. They weren't crabs at all, but simply claws of sweet meat.

"How do I eat these?" inquired Sean.

"You pick out the meat just as you would a crab claw, then dip it into this sauce made from lime and drawn butter," replied the waiter.

Andrea and Sean picked up their seafood forks and dug in. The taste was like sweet crab meat, but the meat was denser. When the Key Lime pie arrived, Andrea joshed to the waiter, "We know how to eat this!"

Andrea commented to Sean, "It looks like a picture out of a cookbook. See how the fluffy white meringue is piled high on top of the lime filling?" As they took their first bite, the tartness of the lime filling made their lips pucker and they laughed at this surprise taste.

With stomachs full and winter coats tossed into the trunk, they finally arrived at Bahia Honda. It didn't take long to register and set up camp. Slathering on more sunscreen they quickly changed into shorts and tees, and set out to explore the island.

A short walk from their campsite took Sean and Andrea to a portion of Flagler's old bridge that jutted out into the Atlantic. Some track remained for campers to walk on and watch the sunset.

After the long ride and delicious lunch, they felt relief and satisfaction at reaching their destination without any major problems. In an embrace, they watched the setting sun go down at the southern most point of the continental United States.

As they lingered on the bridge, they were approached by a couple who looked very tan and relaxed. Sally and Al greeted them like old friends.

"Been here long?" Sally asked, dressed in cut-off jeans and a T-shirt that read 'Margaritaville, Key Weird, FL.' Her husband Al dressed more conservatively in khaki shorts and a golf shirt with the island's famous Cheeca Golf Resort logo.

"My name is Sally and this here, is my husband Al. We've been here for a couple days enjoying this perfect weather."

"We arrived today and are here for Fantasy Fest," said Sean. "Ironically, Philly turned cold just as were getting ready to leave so we are glad to be here in the tropical heat."

"I know what you mean," said Al. He told them they were snowbirds, traveling in their camper between Queens, New York, and Key West. "Bahia Honda is one of our favorite state parks for winter camping."

"Unfortunately, we are working folks," replied Andrea. "Sean is an asset manager for a local bank in Philly and I work in pharmaceutical sales. We decided to take a week's vacation and experience Fantasy Fest. Escaping the beginning of winter is an added bonus."

"We're fantasy bound," injected Sean, "and hope to join the party on Duval Street. We even brought our Halloween costumes. Do you think we should wear them?"

"Of course," said Sally and Al in unison.

Al winked at Sean. "You'll be surprised at the costumes you'll see. Hope you're not embarrassed at nude body paint art."

As if sharing a secret, Sally told them about the real party of Fantasy Fest. She said, "Unlike the bacchanalia of Saturday's Captain Morgan parade with its drunken college kids and outrageous body paint, the parade on Friday night is a neighborhood gathering. Locals wear funky costumes and are very friendly. The Bed and Breakfast Inns set out serving tables with liquor shots, free for the taking. I believe the party starts just before sunset, this coming Friday. You can join the start of the celebration at the old Key West cemetery. We've done it the past few years and it is always a blast! Unfortunately, we are having company this Friday or we would be there. Have fun."

The sun completely disappeared below the horizon. The darkness signaled time for campers to return to their camp sites. The couples said good-night to each other when Andrea had one last thought.

"Can you recommend a place for lunch in Key West?" With a smile, Sally quickly suggested lunch at the Blue Heaven. "It is one of Key West's older establishments in an area known as the Bahamian Village. You'll get a taste of what old Key West was like. When you are there, see the pictures of Ernest Hemingway. It used to be a favorite haunt of his when he lived in Key West back in the early 30s."

Andrea and Sean set Thursday aside for sun bathing, walking on sandy beaches and snorkeling off the shore. They were happy that the beaches were deserted, as if they were on their own private island. Images from the kitchen calendar came alive and they rejoiced in the warmth of the sun and being together. Tomorrow was going to be a day for partying so they wanted to enjoy the solitude of this day. Back at camp, Sean built a fire for s'mores while Andrea made sandwiches with cold-cuts she had in the cooler. First they ate the s'mores, then the sandwiches. After all, they were on vacation. A glass of red wine complemented this unorthodox meal.

Friday morning brought great excitement. Route 1 would take them to the south east end of the continent and "Mile Marker 0." Commemorated by a huge black, white and yellow buoy, it read, "90 Miles to Cuba, Southernmost Point, Continental United States, Key West Florida, and Home of the Sunset." Once there, finding parking was easy but expensive and cost twenty dollars a night. Sean and Andrea didn't care since they were saving money by camping. With the car safely garaged, they checked a local map and headed down Truman Street towards the Bahamian Village and the lunch spot their new friends had recommended, the "Blue Heaven."

The gate to the Bahamian Village Market was wrought iron with a large conch shell centered on top and flanked by upside down bicycle wheels. To Andrea and Sean, it was Key West kitsch at its most eclectic. Local island folk sold jewelry and the familiar red, yellow and green flags of the island waved in the courtyard.

At first, the Blue Heaven proved difficult to find. The area had no fancy B&B's, or souvenir shops. Only run-down, wooden planked homes called "Conch" houses lined the street. Wrap around porches cooled the residences since no air conditioning existed when these homes were built. Andrea thought they didn't look very sturdy, but realized they must be since they weathered many tropical storms. Constructed in the early days of Key West, they housed the Bahamian immigrants who arrived in the Keys to work in the ship salvaging and Cuban cigar making businesses.

On one street corner, a group of dark-skinned, well-built men gathered. They wore beat-up jeans, and sported white muscle shirts that showed their massive strength. Shyly, Andrea asked one of the less intimidating looking men, "Could you please tell me where the Blue Heaven restaurant is?"

"Two blocks, mon," one said pointing up the street. Andrea and Sean hurried off in that direction. As they walked towards the Blue Heaven, roosters strutted their plumage in front of them.

Sean said, "I think they are looking for chickens."

Andrea confessed, "I do feel a little 'chicken' in this unfamiliar neighborhood, but isn't this the kind of adventure we were looking for – unusual and off-beat?"

Large palm trees covered the "Blue" in the "Blue Heaven" sign, showing the restaurant's name as "Heaven."

'This must be the place," exclaimed Andrea, thankful they'd arrived at their destination in this unfamiliar tropical paradise.

Entering the courtyard, they saw the bar. Made of bathtubs cut in half, a wooden plank on top turned them into a bar. Above the bar, a large, weathered water tower rested on a platform. A sign tacked to the water tower read, "Jimmy Buffett played here for cold beers." Across the courtyard, on a make-shift stage, a woman strummed her guitar and sang an unfamiliar song about love in the islands. All around, roosters strutted freely. Andrea wondered out loud, "What is up with all these roosters?"

Sean replied, "Who do you think they belong too? They're everywhere."

Seated at a plain white round table in plastic chairs, they noticed the floor was not sand or broken sea shells that would be common in a tropical restaurant. Instead it was slate. They found out later it originally came from the basement's pool hall. Andrea and Sean were amazed at this bizarre scene.

Their waiter arrived dressed as casually as the surroundings – short, tight jeans, a Blue Heaven T-shirt and flip-flops. "My name is Maurice," he said with an exaggerated gesture putting his hand on his hip. "Here are the menus."

"What do you suggest?" asked Sean.

"It's all very delicious, but the Goombay Gumbo Soup is our specialty."

On Maurice's recommendation, Andrea ordered the soup, and Sean chose the Jamaican Jerk Chicken Sandwich.

Once they placed their order, they walked around to the gift shop. There, hanging on the wall, were pictures of Ernest Hemingway. In one black and white picture, he refereed a boxing match. The clerk said, "Hemingway came here often, especially for the Friday night fights." She explained, "In Blue Heaven's early days, this was a sporting house, bordello, pool hall and cock fighting ring."

Sean imagined Hemingway drinking, flirting, betting and enjoying the "sporting life" he was known for, right here in this very spot. As they left the gift shop, the clerk called out to them, "Check out the graveyard, next to the stage. It is where 'Big Cock' is buried. He was Hemingway's favorite fighting cock. The locals at that time gave the cock one hell of a burial!"

So many thoughts raced through Sean's mind.

He said to Andrea, "Think about it. Pool hall, cock fighting, bordello, boxing ring, Hemingway, Buffett – could this be an abstract 'heaven' that existed in another time?"

Soon after they returned to their table, Maurice brought their lunches. As he put the plates before them, he said, "The Goombay soup is made with okra, tomatoes and peppers. It has a little hot spice for flavor." Turning to Sean, he pointed to his plate and said, "The Jerk chicken is marinated in a secret Blue Heaven recipe and guaranteed to deliver heat." They tasted their dishes at the same time.

"Wow!" exclaimed Sean.

"Wow!" Andrea agreed. "It's enjoyable, but —"

"Hot!" Sean finished her sentence. Washing it down with a cold beer they bid farewell to the dead cock, the quirky waiter and memory of Hemingway.

From "Heaven," they walked past the Winter White House and complex where many Presidents had stayed, beginning with Harry Truman. They laughed when they compared the Heaven experience to politics and what a difference a few short blocks made. From downtown to uptown and from heaven to hell.

Two blocks ahead, they arrived on Duval Street, the main thoroughfare of Key West. All the shops and restaurants displayed Halloween decorations. They stopped at "Sloppy Joe's" for a beer and then on to "Capt'n Tonys" for more beer. The heat of the day made the cold beer especially enjoyable. The streets teemed with college age kids. Ready to party, their excitement for Halloween grew by the hour.

Further down Duval Street, they came upon a costume shop called "Farmville Megastore." The window display had exquisite Halloween costumes. A sign invited the passerby to come inside and live out a fantasy. Entering, the shop buzzed with bizarre activity. Andrea and Sean watched people laughing, trying on costumes and acting out characters. This was not the same as a costume shop found at the suburban mall. It had top quality costumes of every character imaginable. Caught up in this fantasy world and to complement their pirate costumes, Sean bought a replica of a flintlock pistol and Andrea purchased a jewel encrusted saber. Sufficiently armed, they made their way back to the car for a quick change into their costumes, then walked to the cemetery. Taking back streets to get there, Andrea was impressed with the cottage style homes and lovely neighborhood gardens. She thought many of the homes must date back to Flagler's railroad days.

They arrived at the cemetery late in the afternoon. Shadows from the palm trees created eerie designs on the cemetery's headstones. The locals began to gather down Passover Street

"Really, Passover Street?" questioned Sean, as they walked along the cemetery's wall. "The city fathers sure had a sense of humor."

First they saw a group of ladies dressed in hula skirts and bikini tops. They had floral leis twisted in their hair and leis hanging from their necks. Another lady wore a thong. Body painted flowers embellished her bare breasts. On her head was a gold sparkling wig. Sean took a second look. Andrea saw him out of the corner of her eye and jabbed him in the ribs.

"Get use to it," she said. "This is just the beginning of the parade."

More people arrived. One couple carried large cardboards designed to resemble train engines, a tribute to Flagler. The center of the engine was accentuated with hot pink feathers, and glittering stars were strung along the top. The cardboard hung from shoulder straps, like the old sandwich board signs. Underneath the engine appeared leggings of black and pink stripes.

140

In front of them, a group of eight gathered for the march, dressed in blow-up fat suits with hot pink bodices and gold tutus. Crowning their heads were hot pink wigs and gold tiaras. On their feet, sneakers were painted – you guessed it – hot pink. One man's dark brown beard added to the scene's hilarity.

Nestled in a corner among flowering bougainvillea, four Hare Krishna look-alike monks wore orange dyed sheets. Mardi Gras beads hung from their necks and skull caps covered their hair. In character, they chanted the Hare Krishna melody and blessed people as they walked by.

The crowd swelled with interesting costumes, like the person dressed as a white wedding cake, or the elderly, robust man in a pink tutu, a huge multi-colored wig, his face painted up as a clown. They encountered some nudity, but all done in good humor with everyone laughing and having a fun time.

From out of nowhere, two flatbed trucks rolled in. One had a four piece jazz band on it and the other had a Junkanoo band composed of the tradition cow bell, whistle, brass horn and several steel drums with goat skin heads. The crowd divided itself behind either the Jazz or Junkanoo band and the parade started.

Sean and Andrea followed the Junkanoo band feeling the rhythm of the islands, simple but moving. Emboldened by the crowd, Sean unbuttoned his pirate shirt down to his silver skull belt buckle. Andrea hoisted her skirt up and tucked it into her waistband. She then loosened her white linen blouse to reveal a bit more cleavage.

The music carried them on a wave of happiness. They marched behind a man with a T-shirt that read, "We are all here because we are not all there." As their friends on the bridge had told them, white plastic covered tables were set out by the B&Bs, with free liquor shots for the taking. At one point, Sean excused himself to barf behind a hotel's trash bins, but he didn't miss a beat when he joined Andrea. She was dancing with a lady wearing a "Hooter's" T-shirt, orange short shorts, a grey granny wig and round wire-rimmed, rose-colored glasses. As she turned, the back of her T-shirt read, "Old and delightfully tacky yet unrefined retired Hooter," and on her butt was a nuclear symbol patch. Indians, cowboys, g-strings, decorated bare breasts, outlandish green aliens, a Pope, Sting the rock star, all marching and drinking and having a good time. The followers of the Jazz band and the followers of the Junkanoo band came together on Duval Street. A crescendo of costumes, gaiety, music, and beer filled the street.

Andrea and Sean felt themselves slowing down, overwhelmed by too much eye-candy and drink for one night. Turning to head back to the car, Andrea wished that the Junkanoo band would miraculously reappear so she could have a beat for the long walk back. As if by magic, around the corner came the band. Whistles tweeting, drums beating cow bells clanging. Rhythmically, they all marched toward the garage where Andrea and Sean's car was parked.

Saturday morning dawned bright and sunny. It was late morning when Andrea and Sean parked the car in the garage they used the night before. Familiar with the area, they took the short walk to Duval Street. There they found the crowd already gathering on the street for the official parade. As foretold by Sally and Al, the actual Fantasy Fest became a drunken debacle. By noon, beer cans littered the gutters and rude college kids stumbled about. The night temperatures remained warm and crowds lining Duval Street stood six deep. None other than Captain Morgan, a larger than life statue led the parade. Surrounding him were large blow-up bottles of rum, girls in skimpy costumes and leather boots. Behind Captain Morgan, the mile long procession had sea creatures riding bicycles, tall black puppets with scary faces that swooped down into the crowd, a float with a Castro look-a-like shouting, "Viva la Revolucion," banditos riding paper-mache donkeys, and of course, lots of nudity, g-strings and body paint. As the night went on, exhibitionism became too much to witness. After experiencing the Friday night parade, Sean and Andrea felt put-off by the tens of thousands of people pushing and shoving and smelling like yesterday's garbage.

As they prepared to leave the parade and return to the campground, a lady with a tropical scene painted over her well-endowed naked body caught Sean's eye. He left Andrea's side to take a closer look.

In an instant the crowd closed in. Andrea called out his name, frantically trying to find him, when all of sudden she felt herself being lifted into the air and flung over a strong man's shoulder. Looking down, she could see black leather boots that went up to his knees and baggy black and white striped pants. From his waist flowed a red sash that tucked in his sword. Andrea couldn't believe it. A pirate had kidnapped her.

"Let me down," she screamed and tried to kick her abductor. "What do you think you're doing? This isn't funny!" she protested. Apparently, the crowd thought this an act and applauded the pirate's audacity.

He carried her for a few blocks with her kicking and screaming the whole way. He grunted, then said, "Stop strugglin' or I'll have to beat ye wit' a cat o' nine tales. I be taken ye to our ship that flies the Jolly Roger."

Andrea fell back as the pirate walked up a slanted gang plank. She looked down at the floor below and saw it was similar to the planks found on a boat's deck. In fact, the boat revealed itself to be a pirate boat float, its sails hoisted to parade down Duval Street. Her captor put her down and shoved her off to another pirate.

"Who be this lady?" asked one of the pirates.

"Can't sail wit' only twelve wenches as crew. We need thirteen if we be carrying them on board. Or bad luck be sending us down to Davey Jones' locker," he replied.

Because of the authenticity of Andrea's costume, the rogue pirate thought Andrea would complement the crew. Every Key West pirate knows it is an honor to sail aboard a ship carrying the Conch Republic flag. In the holiday spirit, he had captured her.

"Aye, she be like a princess, wit' all her finery," said one of the wenches as she handed Andrea a mug of rum and cookies made to look like "hard-tack."

"Me name is Anne Bonny and tis' here be Mary Read. Maybe ye' heard of us?" asked one of the wenches.

Andrea knew the names well. There were feared female pirates that roamed the Caribbean seas along with Blackbeard and Captain Morgan, pilfering towns and robbing the rich. Not bad company, she thought.

Everyone treated Andrea as an old shipmate until they realized she didn't know the language or how to fight with her sword.

"Who be this person?" they asked.

"I'm a tourist from Philly and not part of your Conch Republic Pirate Brigade, although you do have a nice boat," she meekly responded.

"It be no boat me' lady, but a ship," said one of the pirates. Then he put his arm around Andrea and explained their need for a thirteenth person.

"Another lady was suppose to show up, but never did," he said. They were desperate for crew and this was, after all, Fantasy Fest. Poor Andrea's fantasy was not working out because she missed Sean. She explained to the crew how she got separated from Sean. The pirates began to hatch a plan.

Slowly, the ship started rolling, with music blaring, and swords a-blazing. By watching the others, Andrea learned how to dramatically swing her sword and got into the fantasy of being a pirate. Besides, there wasn't much that Andrea could do but drink rum and enjoy herself. If she didn't see Sean, then she hoped to meet him later that evening at the car.

About two blocks into the parade, Andrea spotted Sean searching for her. She pointed him out to the Captain, and their plan unfolded. "No problem matey," he said and ordered that the gang plank be positioned to reach the street. Andrea hid and when they were abreast of Sean, they rolled out the plank.

"Look ye thar at me new wench, ye land lubbin' scallywag. Bet ye pay a piece o' eight fer what we got on thee' poop deck," shouted the pirate.

With much fanfare and cursing, the pirates revealed the conspirator on the ship - Andrea. Sean was shocked to see her. "Shiver me timbers!" he yelled. "Ye got the wrong wench!" and bounded up the gangplank into Andrea's arms.

The crowd yelled, "Walk the plank. Walk the plank!" Excited to see each other, they hugged and kissed and the crowd screamed wildly. Sean accepted a swig of rum before the brigade sailed down Duval Street, throwing beads to the crowd.

Thus ended Andrea and Sean's trip to paradise. Before they left Bahia Honda, their iPhone reported sunny weather and 40 degrees in Philly. They laughed and Sean said, "Well at least it was warming up."

Andrea hugged Sean, decorated him with some beads she had kept, and replied, "No matter how cold it gets, we've got our tans and memories to keep us warm."

Sean agreed and said, "Don't forget, there are many more adventures to be had. In the meantime, hot rum will keep us warm through the coming winter. Our tropical paradise is only a memory away."

A PERFECT UNION

by

Ruth Duncan

Bruce sipped his gin and tonic as he gazed at the tropical sunset from the balcony of his hotel suite. Waikiki Beach stretched out before him toward Diamond Head. He'd carefully chosen The Moana Hotel, the celebrated "First Lady of Waikiki" since 1901, to be the luxury destination for his honeymoon. Yet, here he stood, alone.

At the last minute, Leslie canceled coming with him. Bruce had tried hard to smooth things over. "Just because my parents, the high and almighty Armstrongs, won't approve of our marriage doesn't mean it's finished between us," he'd pleaded, "and it doesn't mean we still can't take our trip together."

But Leslie wouldn't waver. They'd argued for weeks about it. "If I'm not good enough for you to marry, then I'm not good enough to go on some fake honeymoon either!"

So, in the end, Bruce boarded the plane by himself. Besides his travel package being non-refundable, he also thought he needed some time away from L.A. and his work at the bank. His forty-first birthday loomed close, so he decided where better than the paradise of Hawaii to rethink how he would survive in the years ahead without Leslie in his life.

He remembered the events leading up to this predicament. It all began when he introduced Leslie to his parents. He'd kept everything under wraps for the entire six months they'd been dating, because when he was honest with himself, he knew what their reaction would be and he didn't know how to solve his dilemma. He couldn't give Leslie up, but he couldn't go against his parents either, especially his father.

That fateful Saturday, in his gleaming red Ferrari Enzo, Bruce had driven Leslie to his parent's Bel Air mansion. He parked in the shade beneath the porte-cochere. "Wait here a few minutes while I go inside?"

Leslie didn't understand. "They're expecting us, aren't they?"

"Yes, but give me a moment with them first. As I told you, the Armstrong family isn't the easiest to deal with."

"Is there a problem?"

"No, no, not at all," Bruce gave his reassurance, wishing he felt as confident as he was trying to sound. "I'll be back for you in a few minutes."

Bruce rang the doorbell, then inserted his key and let himself in. His mother, Judy Armstrong, quickly came down the grand staircase into the foyer to greet him. "Come here and see your momma," she said. "How's my baby boy?"

"Fine, Mom," Bruce cringed. "I'm doing fine." He threw his arms around her and gave her the big bear hug he knew she expected. His mother almost equaled his six foot height, and with their bleached blonde hair, golden tans, and toned, athletic bodies, they represented the Southern California lifestyle to perfection.

"I'm so pleased we're finally going to meet Leslie. I can't believe you've kept us in the dark for so long. Of course, I really want to weep that I'm losin' you to someone else, but I'm also trying to be happy and think about the wedding." She paused and looked around. "But where is Leslie? Already gone in to meet Daddy?"

Bruce laughed his nervous laugh. "No, no, Leslie's still in my car, but I wanted to have you both to myself for a minute. I need to explain something first."

"Well, honey," she said, patting his cheek with her bejeweled fingers, "then let's go find Daddy. I think he's in the library."

Bruce dreaded going into his least favorite room of the house. For him, the library's dark walls, massive mahogany furniture, and musty books created a dungeon-like feel. As a child, his mother had always marched him in there for his father to mete out punishments for his misbehaviors. Bruce didn't remember anything good ever happening in that room in all his forty years of memory, but he hoped today might be different.

As they entered, Jack Armstrong rose from his leather chair, carefully balanced his martini, and came forward to shake his son's hand. "Good to see you," he said. "I've had some concerns about our new Tampa office and wanted to tell you what I think. Now, with you as the new region's vice-president—"

"Jack, honey," Judy interrupted, "not right now. Leslie's stashed outside waitin' to come in and meet us. You'll have to talk all your banking stuff later." She smiled at her husband with the southern charm that had attracted him in the beginning and still held his interest. "I can't wait a moment longer. It's really naughty of Bruce to keep us in such suspense."

"All right, all right," Jack conceded. "Marriage news first, but then it's my turn to talk business with Bruce."

"There's something I need to tell you though," Bruce began. "I know how you both have your hearts set on a big Hollywood style wedding, but—"

"For God's sake, Bruce," his father thundered, "you can talk about all that crap with your momma some other time. Go get Leslie and let's get on with this."

Bruce tried again. "But I need you to know . . ." His voice weakened as his father's withering look cut off his words, controlling him no differently from when he'd been ten years old. Bruce glanced at his mother, but she had retreated into her usual support-my-husband-no-matter-what pattern, also no different from when he'd been ten.

Bruce turned on his heel and walked out to the car. "Just let them be surprised," he muttered.

Hand in hand, the two lovers came inside the house, laughing at a small private joke between them, as they entered the library. The parents stood in front of the stone fireplace, stiffly formal, as if practicing for the wedding reception line.

"Mom, Dad," Bruce said, "this is Leslie, the man I love and plan to marry." Bruce's father wilted significantly from his usual regal stance crafted as President of Century Bank, the largest financial institution on the west coast. Though close to retirement age, he prided himself on his youthful appearance and strong grip on life.

"Believe this calls for a very stiff one," he said to no one in particular and headed for the bar in the corner of the room.

"Oh . . . oh . . . oh my god," Bruce's mom choked out, as she collapsed into a nearby Louis Vuitton settee.

Bruce's dad began, "So, this is the one who's going to take our little Bruce away from us, is it?"

Everyone smiled in the polite way the Armstrong's had practiced for generations, their stiff upper-lip persona tracing back to the ancestral days of their family at the Royal Court of England.

Bruce noticed his Dad didn't shake Leslie's hand, didn't offer them drinks, or even invite them to sit down. He glanced at Leslie who seemed oblivious to these slights. Leslie's positive attitude, reflected in his favorite saying, "Surf's up, Dude! It's a great day!" often protected him from life's negative bumps.

"Well," Jack continued, "I guess we're going to have to adjust our thinking from *losing* a son to *gaining* a son." He nodded to Bruce. "Why don't you take your mother out to the gardens so I can have a word with Leslie?"

Bruce reached his hand out to his mother, lifted and then half carried her from the room. He glanced back at Leslie and his father, and felt the gloom of the library closing in on his lover. Bruce breathed a prayer that Leslie's openness and enthusiasm, qualities that he loved, would also somehow charm his father.

After his wife and son were out of sight, Jack sat down behind his imposing desk and motioned Leslie to take the chair directly across from him. The Prosecutor and the Witness. "Now," he said, "I need to know a few things about you. First, how old are you?"

"Twenty-six. You probably think I'm too young, and to be honest, I never dated an old guy before. But then I met Bruce, and we make each other very happy, and I think we're really good for each other."

"Hmmm," Jack responded, "and what's your career?"

"Oh, I don't have a job. I've been going to college."

"And what university would that be?"

"The School for Life Experiences. Down in Laguna Beach. I guess you heard it got shut down by some state regulators, so right now I'm kind of between things. Don't worry though. I love nature and flowers and green stuff and Bruce says he's going to buy me a flower shop to run. That's always been a dream of mine and I'm going to name it *Flowers by Leslie*. With Bruce's job at the bank, he says he can get me all the money I'll need to get started."

* * * * *

Early the next morning, Bruce received a text from his dad.

No VP job if you cont. w/
that kid. Maybe NO job at all.
Board meets Fri. Let me no ur
decision.

Bruce had faced the issue with accountant like precision, weighing the options of a silver-spoon-in-his-mouth lifestyle versus companionship, love and fun with Leslie. He wanted both, but for now, he couldn't figure out a solution. He felt his soul being ripped out by his father, but in the end, decided he had no real choice but to continue with his career at the bank.

* * * * *

Standing alone on the balcony of his honeymoon suite, Bruce missed Leslie, feeling like only half a person without his other half to share the trip they'd planned together with such joy and anticipation. He clutched the railing and stared down at the vacationing couples and families gathering for dinner in the courtyard below. That should have been us, he thought, and began second-guessing his decision to give up on Leslie and come to Hawaii alone.

Within the year, he'd be moving to Tampa and opening the new office of Century Bank for the southeast region. He recognized the opportunity his dad and the Board had given him, but he also knew the challenges, long hours, and stress that awaited him. And now, he was expected to do it all without Leslie by his side. It was Leslie's youthful, carefree outlook that had helped take the edge off when situations got too chaotic at work.

Now, Leslie wouldn't even answer his phone calls, so Bruce quit calling him. But he continued to text Leslie every day, usually in the mornings when he first woke up as that's when he missed Leslie the most. He could only hope his messages were being read. It helped Bruce keep a glimmer of optimism that a connection remained between them.

The sun disappeared below the horizon, broadcasting streaks of gold across the water and lighting the sky with magenta and crimson as if it were on fire. Bruce wished he'd seen the mythical flash of green light that sometimes appeared as the sun dipped below the water's edge. Island lore guaranteed that sighting the green light brought immediate good luck. However, Bruce reminded himself that he had thirteen more sunsets, thirteen more chances, to see the magic and collect his good luck before he returned to the mainland.

As Bruce turned to go inside, he noticed a woman had appeared on the adjacent balcony. With only a trellis of fuchsia colored bougainvillea separating them, he could easily see her. She appeared thirty-something, with a blonde ponytail trailing down her back. A lei of plumerias encircled her neck, identical to the ones greeters present to tourists at the Oahu airport. Like him, she'd probably just arrived on the island. He waited a few moments, wanting to hear if anyone was with her. When he heard nothing, he called to her, "Hello next door neighbor. Did you arrive in time to see the sunset?"

"Spectacular, wasn't it?" she answered. "That red and purple palette reminded me of a Simon Kee painting."

"You know Simon Kee's work? I saw his exhibit at the Soho gallery in L.A. last month—"

"Really?" she interrupted. "Me too and I absolutely loved it." Her words bubbled along. "OMG, you're from L.A. too?"

They shared some of their city experiences and laughed at their similar likes and dislikes. Bruce found himself quite entertained by her and wanting to know her better.

After a few minutes, he said, "We can't talk through this trellis all night. How'd you like to get some dinner? My treat. Down in the courtyard beneath the famous Banyan tree?"

"Sure," she laughed, "but I need you to know something first. I'm a lesbian, here to have a get-over-being-dumped vacation. So, if you're looking for romance, I'm not the one. Maybe you want to take your invitation back?"

"Absolutely not. Actually, I think we're pretty well suited to be friends," Bruce said, "but let's start at the beginning. What's your name?"

"Piper," she said, "Piper Ellis."

"Well, Piper, I'm Bruce Armstrong and we have more in common than you know. Let's go get some dinner."

* * * * *

After two weeks in the islands, neither could remember how life had been before they'd met each other. They toured all the tourist attractions together starting with Pearl Harbor. They threw roses into the "Black Tears," patches of oil still seeping to the surface at the Arizona Memorial, and listened to their tour guide, a World War II veteran, tell his memories of the Day of Infamy. When they climbed down into the USS Bowfin submarine, claustrophobia overcame Piper and she nearly trampled Bruce to run back up the exit stairs into the fresh air. Every day they laughed over her new-found phobia and Bruce enjoyed embellishing the tale with each retelling.

They snorkeled among brilliant yellow butterfly fish and green sea turtles in the shallow waters of Hanauma Bay, until a Moray eel popped out of its coral reef home and scared Piper back to shore. They took an outrigger canoe ride, something unique to Waikiki Beach, and had their photo taken while they paddled away, like any happy vacationing couple. On an island hopping trip to Maui, they rode bicycles down the Haleakala Crater Trail from its 10,000 foot summit. Bruce could not believe what a perfect companion Piper was. Everything he enjoyed doing she loved too, and her happiness and penchant for laughing freely and often energized him. Every day, Bruce looked forward to spending time with her. Through all of their adventures, they talked and talked.

Bruce found it easy to tell Piper about his feelings of loss and grief from being forced to give Leslie up, and his anger at the intolerance and control exercised by his parents. Eventually Bruce found himself talked out, having gone over every detail of the breakup at least twice, and in some cases, multiple times. Piper, on the other hand, remained quite silent about being "dumped," as she'd put it when she first met Bruce. Except for a few brief mentions of what someone named Mandy would have said, liked or disliked about something they'd encountered, Piper avoided the subject.

On the last day of their vacation, they dined on Oahu's North Shore at Jameson's By the Sea, a kitschy restaurant famous for its location across the road from world class surfing. They sat outdoors on weathered stools grouped around a worn plank table. Despite the change in season, strands of Christmas lights twinkled on the arbor beams above them. Across the sand, they watched surfers catch their final waves of the day.

Bruce ordered Blue Hawaii drinks for them and toasted Piper. "Here's to a Springtime Christmas in Hawaii!"

Piper held her glass up against the rays of the setting sun. "The Curacao liqueur colors the drink the same lovely blue that my wedding dress was. Sitting here with you makes it hard to believe I almost got married last month."

"You actually had set the date?"

"More than that," Piper answered. "We were literally right at the altar of the San Francisco City Clerk's office. Mandy had the marriage license in her hands, and we were standing around with other couples in a reception room waiting our turn. I felt so full of happiness, thinking my dream of marrying Mandy was actually coming true. She looked so great in her tuxedo and I loved my dress. Everything's perfect, and then all of a sudden, Mandy just ripped up the license. 'I can't go through with it,' she said. For a moment, I simply stood there, still smelling the sweet gardenias in my bouquet, not really comprehending what had just happened. I think I finally whispered, 'What?'."

"You must have been devastated. At least Leslie and I hadn't gotten to that stage. What did you do? Did you find out why she changed her mind?"

"Mandy took me by the shoulder, pushed me out into the hallway, and told me she'd recently found another woman she realized she loved more than me, her 'true soul mate' she said, so she couldn't go through with our ceremony."

"Wow, that's brutal, coming at the last minute like that," Bruce sympathized.

"It gets worse," Piper said. "She walked out of the building and left me standing there in a city I didn't know, and without any way to get back to L.A. I had to negotiate BART all by myself to find a car rental agency and then drive down the Coast Highway alone. I cried most of the way, about nine hours worth. But, I haven't cried one tear since.

"It's only been a month, but I realize now that I was so fortunate Mandy didn't go through with it." Piper leaned across the table and held Bruce's hand. "Your making me feel so special, all the happy times we've had — and no arguments — that's a big thing, believe me. It puts the whole experience I had with Mandy in an entirely different perspective. You have no idea how much you've helped me."

"I really didn't know what you've been thinking about," Bruce said. "I assumed you were having a hard time, the same way I'm missing Leslie. So if that's not the case, good for you! That's great!"

Piper laughed. "Actually I'm more mad than sad. Mandy left me in a real mess. I'd already given up my apartment lease because I was going to live in her house, and you know how hard it is to find a place to rent at any reasonable price in L.A. Plus, I'm between movie projects right now. Some would call it unemployed. I know I'll get another script writing job, I always do, but meanwhile . . . homeless and jobless, that's me."

"That's a lot to handle," Bruce said. "Let's order something extravagant off the menu, and take a walk on the beach to enjoy our last night in the islands. Maybe you can forget your worries, for now anyway."

"You're right. Tomorrow will be here too soon and there'll be plenty of time to worry then."

* * * * *

Bruce and Piper settled into their airline seats, first class upgrades at Bruce's insistence. "It's terrific that you got my reservation changed and we're able to fly back together," Piper said. "Thank you so much." She leaned over and gave him a kiss on his cheek. "Meeting you was my lucky day."

Bruce smiled. "No, it was *my* lucky day. And I never even had to see that damned green light at sundown that's supposed to bring all the good fortune." He ordered mai-tais from the flight attendant. "Fresh pineapple slices on the side, please."

"Not quite ready to give up the island life?" Piper teased. The sweet fruit had become a staple of their diet. "Hard to believe today's our last day in paradise, the last day we'll spend together."

"I've been thinking about that," Bruce said. "I told you about my house in Brentwood, but I didn't mention that I also have a pool house. It's sitting there empty, waiting for you to move in, if you'd like. I thought about everything you said last night and you're totally welcome to use it."

Piper stared at Bruce, wide eyes filled with tears that soon overflowed down her cheeks. "Really?" she managed to say. "You'd do that for me?"

Bruce dabbed at her tears with his cocktail napkin. "Everything's going to be just fine," he said. "Don't worry. I'll take care of you."

* * * * *

In Los Angeles, Bruce returned to work, taking over the development plans for opening the new Century Bank Tower in downtown Tampa, where he'd soon oversee all operations in seven southeastern states. Piper moved into his pool house and landed a contract to adapt Jonathan Sever's bestselling novel, *The Beginning*, into a movie. Sometimes, depending on their schedules, Bruce's housekeeper, Carmen, served them dinner outside by the pool, or they dined at one of the pricey restaurants on Rodeo Drive or at the famed Lawry's on La Cienega. On the weekends when Bruce didn't work, they visited museums, the Getty being their favorite, or roller bladed on Venice Beach. For dress-up events, Piper became the lady on Bruce's arm at charity functions.

Several months passed, and their relationship blossomed into a dynamic that neither Bruce nor Piper had experienced before. On the weekends, they explored the southern California landscape together, from the Saddleback Mountains to Palm Springs' casinos to the many art galleries of La Jolla. Their lives might have continued on the same track if their relationship hadn't become a public item.

At the annual Rescuing Unwanted Furry Friends (RUFF) fundraiser in Laguna Beach, the paparazzi caught them on camera, Bruce in an Armani tux and Piper in a knock-off Chanel gown. That weekend the Sunday Out and About section of the L.A. Times featured their photo as the Celebrity Couple of the Week. Before noon, Bruce's mother had already phoned him, and when he didn't pick up, left a message demanding answers to her version of the game, "20 Questions."

* * * * *

Piper sat in the shade of the cabana by Bruce's pool, her iPad cradled in her lap. She had spent her Sunday afternoon developing several scenes of intense dialogue for her film project. Getting into the minds and emotions of her characters exhausted her. She closed her case and set it aside, leaned back on the lounge chair, rubbed her forehead and closed her eyes.

Bruce watched Piper from his kitchen window. "Carmen, I think she's ready to quit for the day. Let's go." With the newspaper tucked under his arm, Bruce carried a pitcher of margaritas and glasses. Carmen trailed behind him, balancing plates of quesadillas, mini-burritos and tacos.

"It's five o'clock somewhere," Bruce called out as they approached Piper, "and I've brought peach margaritas and munchies to celebrate."

After they sampled their margaritas, Bruce quietly said, "My mom called this morning and gave me hell. "

"Hell for what?"

Bruce crunched on a taco. "For not telling her about you. More specifically, for not telling her about *us*." He handed her the newspaper, folded to show their featured photo. "Mom's fixated on the title of 'Couple'."

Piper scrutinized the article and then laughed. "A good picture of us, don't you think? But doesn't she realize you'd never be interested in me *that* way?"

"Hope springs eternal in the Armstrong household, I guess. Both Mom and Dad are probably still praying everyday that I'll 'discover' girls. You'd think my introducing Leslie to them would have made them realize the facts of my life, but I guess it didn't."

"Maybe," Piper mused, "because you gave in to your dad's ultimatum of choosing his bank over Leslie?"

"Maybe," Bruce agreed, "or more likely, they've decided to close their minds to who I am, like they've done all my life. I've tried to live my own way before, but I always seem to be pulled back into their web. Especially after I took the bank job. I wonder what they'd do if I just . . ." Bruce cut off his thought, seeming to abandon the dark subject he'd been headed toward, and instead turned his attention to Piper. "Do you miss Mandy at all?"

"Absolutely not." Piper grimaced for a moment before her familiar, happy smile broke through. "You've helped me rediscover who I am and how much fun life can be." She raised her glass in a toast to Bruce. "Let's drink to a future bringing great things for both of us."

Bruce freshened Piper's margarita and poured himself another glass. "Carmen makes the best margaritas ever, doesn't she? I've asked her to come work for me in Tampa when I move."

"Oh," Piper responded in a soft voice, tentative and small, unlike her usual demeanor. "I guess I need to be making plans to get out of here. When's this going to happen?"

"The house will be on the market in a few days. If it doesn't sell in a couple of months, the bank will buy me out. On my last trip to Tampa I rented an exec condo. So the move will be in a couple of months at the most."

Piper stared at the waterfall cascading into the pool drawing her spirit down with it. She finished her drink and stood up.

Bruce leaned toward her and grasped her wrist. "Don't go. I have something important to ask you." Piper perched on the edge of her chair as if ready to flee at any moment.

Bruce took both of her hands in his. "I want you to come to Tampa with me. And I want you to marry me." He paused, hoping to see the reaction he so much desired. "Will you marry me, Piper?"

* * * * *

Over the next few days, Bruce and Piper discussed the details of their "arrangement," as Piper preferred to call it instead of a marriage. She certainly saw the financial stability, the luxurious lifestyle to which she had so easily become accustomed and readily admitted how Bruce's plan would benefit and satisfy her.

"But Bruce, I still don't see what you'd gain by taking me on. Even with a pre-nupt agreement to protect your assets, you know I'm still not going to be able to contribute much toward household expenses. So what's in it for you?"

"I've just never known anyone like you before, Bruce explained. "You're like the sister I never had – no, you're more than that – and I just don't ever want to be without you. I'm thinking my chasing guys days were highly overrated. But I promise you that you can still lead your own separate life if that's what you want.

"Plus, my parents will be ecstatic and so will the bank. It'll make my life so much easier. The pressure to settle down and have a family will be gone. By the way, how do you feel about kids?"

"Actually, I think I might like one or two. But maybe we better try adopting a dog first to see if we can get the hang of it."

* * * * *

Once Bruce had Piper's agreement, he called his mother with answers for her bundle of questions. Now armed with all the details, Judy Armstrong immediately broke the wedding news to her husband.

Jack counted off on his fingers all the information he'd just been told. "A girl, an English sounding name, a blonde, 32 years old, educated and employed. Sounds too good to be true. When do we get to meet her?"

After the Leslie fiasco at his parents' home, Bruce chose the neutral territory of Duke's restaurant on the beach in Malibu to introduce Piper. Named after the famed Olympic swimmer and surfer, Duke Kahanamoku, the Aloha spirit began at the door with hostess, Gidget of the TV series, greeting them. They were shown to a table on the open deck with gorgeous views of the Channel Islands and Catalina. While Bruce and his mother scrutinized the menu, Jack quizzed Piper. It was questionable whether her education at Wellesley or her screenwriting credits impressed him the most.

Finally, Judy said, "Jack, she's not on the witness stand. You need to quit the third degree."

"Maybe he's going to write my biography," Piper joked, as she picked up her menu. "Be sure to include that Duke's hula pie is my favorite dessert. Macadamia ice cream with a chocolate crust. Mmm, now that's really living, don't you think?"

"Be careful, Dad," Bruce warned. "As you speak, she's probably writing you into a script as a character even grumpier than ol' Scrooge himself."

"I always have a quandary in character development," Piper laughed. "Will he be the good guy with a little bit of villainy buried somewhere inside him, or a blackheart with a smidgen of hidden goodness? Every story searches for that balance, the yin and yang of life. Finding a satisfying contrast is always the challenge.

"You'll have to stop me when I start talking about my writing though, otherwise I'll just go on and on forever. It's my passion and I tend to get carried away . . ."

"Nonsense," Jack replied. "It's great that you love your career. Actually," he raised his eyebrows and turned to his wife, "we're delighted that you actually *have* a career. Aren't we, Judy?"

"Absolutely," Judy chimed in. "We're so pleased to meet you, dear, and welcome you into our family. Now tell me about your engagement ring. From here, it shouts 'Harry Winston' all over. Am I right?"

Piper held out her left hand and revealed a five carat canary yellow diamond set in platinum on her ring finger. "You're right," she said. "Bruce said he wanted the very best for me. It's gorgeous, isn't it?"

"Son, I'm so proud of you," Jack leaned back in his chair, as if presiding over the gathering and seeming to take credit for the turn in events. "You're finally doing things the right way. None of that nonsense from the past." He turned to Piper. "If you have any problems with this guy, you let me know. Keep him honest. Right?"

Piper felt Bruce's body tense up beside her. "Sure," she agreed with her future father-in-law, "but I don't think I'll need any help."

"Just make sure he treats you right," Jack added, and with this sort of an admonition, Piper wasn't sure exactly what hidden message he may have been trying to convey to her. She decided that later she'd ask Bruce what his father had *really* been trying to tell her.

Oblivious to the undercurrent at the table, Judy continued to ooh and aah over the sparkling treasure on Piper's finger. "Jack, we have an anniversary coming up. You may have to visit Harry Winston's too."

When Piper told her future mother-in-law that her own mother had died fifteen years earlier, and that she'd lost contact with her dad who was busy with a new wife and family somewhere in Ohio, Judy immediately expressed sympathy for Piper's loss. Then she floated off again into visions of wedding planning bliss. Never having a daughter of her own, she realized her dream of being the mother of the bride might still come true.

"Bruce and I decided we want a destination wedding," Piper beamed, "and where better than our new home state of Florida. Bruce booked the Don CeSar Resort in St. Pete Beach for the first Saturday of December. It's been called 'the pink castle' since the 1920s and reminds us of the Royal Hawaiian, 'the pink lady' of Waikiki Beach, a hotel that we loved so much."

Bruce saw the dismay on his mother's face when she heard the wedding wouldn't be in L.A., but also noted how quickly she covered her feelings as Piper presented her with a lengthy to-do list.

"I need your help with the invitations, the caterer, the photographer, music. I don't even know what all. I'm sure you know a lot more about these things than I do, so whatever you choose will be great – or else, ask Bruce. Whatever he wants will be just fine with me."

Bruce nodded. "Sure, mom, just give me a call."

"My time's really limited," Piper continued. "I've got to finish my script. I absolutely can't miss my deadline, so I'm already feeling pressured."

"What about your wedding gown? Your bridesmaids?" Judy inquired.

"I've asked my very best girlfriends, DeeDee and Madison, to be in the wedding and we can all take off work for an afternoon to shop. You'll go with us to choose the dresses, won't you?"

"Absolutely." Judy's eyes sparkled and Bruce could almost hear his mother's organizational cogs churning. He knew she was the party planner extraordinaire. "Do you have a designer in mind," she ventured, "so I can schedule an appointment?"

"I've been a T.J. Maxx shopper for such a long time . . . so I don't know, but I suppose if you want a real designer, then Vera Wang's great, or Caroline Herrera. You pick. I've seen their clothes on movie sets and they all look fantastic to me. Keep in mind I'm not a frou-frou kind of girl and the wedding's on the beach."

Bruce put his arm around Piper's shoulders and leaned in closer to his mother. "There is one thing I want to take care of. I'll order the flowers in Tampa so I can actually see them firsthand and make sure they're fresh."

"Well, I'm surprised you're interested in flowers," Judy began, "but—"

Jack interrupted. "Hey, it's their wedding. Bruce can handle it."

Piper laughed and turned to her future father-in-law. "He really can! In Hawaii, Bruce was like a horticulturist - making lists, studying all the island's flowers, talking to growers. Bruce, maybe we could have orchid leis for all the guests?"

* * * * *

The evening before the wedding, DeeDee and Madison flew in from L.A. in time for the rehearsal. Piper had introduced them to each other on a movie set several years before, and now, they were a committed couple. Before their shopping trip for wedding dresses with Bruce's mother, Piper had cautioned her bridesmaids not to give off any clues about their sexuality to her future in-laws. After their day together with Judy had gone without incident, Piper's anxiety lessened. She felt they would easily stay under the Armstrong's lesbian radar.

After the wedding rehearsal, limos took the Armstrongs and some of their California guests, along with the wedding party, to dinner at Island Breeze, a trendy club on Tampa Bay's inland waterway. Judy's party lasted for hours. Her planning expanded beyond the menu to include imported hula dancers and a band to play, "Dreams come true in Blue Hawaii."

Afterwards, everyone returned to the Don CeSar. DeeDee, Madison, and Piper gathered in the bride's suite of rooms. They settled themselves on the living room couches and as girlfriends do, talked far into the morning hours.

To Piper's surprise, both of her friends questioned her decision to marry Bruce. Madison had been especially insistent.

"Are you sure you can trust Bruce? Will he drop you like Mandy did if Leslie shows up? And then where will you be? Stranded in Florida? That'll be a lot worse than having to drive down the Pacific Coast Highway by yourself."

Piper didn't hesitate. "Bruce me he's not had any contact with Leslie for many months. I'm sure that's long over. I do think I can trust him. He said he'd take care of me and he even said he's kind of given up on guys."

"Really?" Madison frowned. "I wouldn't be too sure about that."

Piper shrugged. "I don't know. That's just what he said."

Madison continued, "And what about your writing? How are you going to find script jobs when you're not able to network Hollywood?"

"That's another plus of this arrangement," Piper explained. "Instead of adapting other people's books, I'm going to have the financial freedom to write my own original screenplays."

Madison shook her head slowly. "I'm only saying that less than a year ago, you were giving up everything to move in with Mandy – partly for security – and I hate to remind you how well that worked out. Are you doing this for – and I hate to say this – for the money? Do you really think Bruce is being honest with you and that you can trust him?"

Madison stood up, stretched her arms above her head, and yawned. "It's your life. You know we love you, so this is the last time I'll ever bring this subject up. Tomorrow, if you decide to go ahead, we're absolutely going to be your rah-rah team. Right, DeeDee?"

DeeDee didn't answer. She was curled up in the corner of a sofa, sound asleep. Madison gently shook her awake, and after goodnights, hugs and kisses for Piper, they left to sleep the few remaining hours before dawn in their own room down the hall.

* * * * *

The early morning sunshine streamed through the French doors of Piper's room, promising a warm Florida day for her December wedding. While much of the country struggled with freezing rain and snow, the forecast for Tampa Bay predicted 82 perfect degrees for the afternoon.

Piper dressed quickly in shorts and a tee, went downstairs, out the back doors past the swimming pools, and onto the sparkling white sand for a quick stroll. She wanted to walk on the beach, sort things out and clear her head, and especially think through some of the doubts Madison had posed the evening before.

She stood in the chilly Gulf waters feeling the rhythm of the waves lapping her legs, lapping the shore, returning to swish around her ankles again and again. Tiny whirlpools swirled about her and the sand sucked at her toes. She kicked at the water, and looked toward the horizon as if an answer to her questions might appear.

Piper waded further down the beach, and then felt the warm sand under her feet as she walked back out of the water. Her engagement ring sparkled in the sunshine, a reminder of Bruce's commitment to her. Everything he'd ever told her, everything he'd promised he would do – she couldn't remember anything he'd ever not been honest about. Piper did wish she had asked Bruce about whatever his dad had been trying to tell her on that first day she'd met his family. Somehow she'd never found a time to question Bruce; it just had never come up again, so she reasoned it must have been nothing.

She held out her hand again to admire her huge gem. Of course, she could trust Bruce. He was honest, her best friend, and she felt foolish about doubting her decision to go forward with their plans.

Piper glanced at her Rolex, another luxurious gift from Bruce. Eight o'clock already. She realized it was time to walk back to the hotel and begin her new life as a soon-to-be married woman. A large white delivery truck pulled onto the beach about fifty yards ahead of her and parked directly behind the hotel. "Blue's Rentals," the side panel read. Several guys in blue uniforms leaped out, opened the rear doors, and began unloading pallets of white folding chairs.

She was surprised that preparation for her afternoon ceremony had already begun. It was an indication of how a simple beach wedding had turned into a several hundred guest extravaganza orchestrated by Judy Armstrong. Piper smiled. Who would have thought that putting Bruce's mom in charge of the wedding would have made her future mother-in-law so thrilled and viewing Piper as her new best friend?

Piper continued up the walkway to the front entrance of the hotel. She stopped suddenly, her heart pounding as she saw another delivery truck parked in the hotel's circular drive. Along with a brightly colored bouquet of Hawaiian styled flowers painted on the truck's side, the fancy cursive script read, *Flowers by Leslie*.

LIFE BEHIND THE GATES

by

Maureen Lacey

Our Pennsylvania house stands on the southeast corner of the block, grand, with large white columns and ornate trim. The front lawn is surrounded by hydrangeas forced to bloom in abundance by the daily addition of coffee grounds from my husband's biggest vice. This refuge has been our home for the past twenty plus years. Three babies were raised here along with dogs, cats and a collection of strays, some two-legged, others four, but all welcome.

I recall these favorite memories while I watch the movers juggle lamps, baskets and other comforts of what we'd soon call, "the old house." *How do I feel about this move? It's hard to say, but too late to turn back.* When we move forward, how much of ourselves do we leave behind? Do we gather all our memories into the little packing boxes of our thoughts to be rescued when needed or smothered when time shuns their reappearance? I am thrilled we are not paying by the pound to move our memories. Who could afford the grand total?

The good-bye party last night was a time to rediscover old friendships and promise to write, call or visit. I know these pledges were true but not practical. Time and distance are barriers we have learned to dance with on many occasions.

The last of the boxes has been loaded onto the moving van and I return to walk through the old house one last time. Opening the glass front door, I stand on the threshold to the foyer and look around tentatively, like a stranger. The tears blur my vision, but after a quick wipe with my sleeve, I follow the path past the living room and dining room to the kitchen and the back of the house. I stop, and standing in the middle of the kitchen, I am captured by the sunshine and its magical dance on the floor tiles. Swirls of light, of color reminiscent of the energy painted by this grown family. We have been together so long it only seems natural that I speak out loud to the kitchen. Good friends are just like us. They feed each other, keep each other warm, and offer a beautiful view of things to be discovered. With this wrap of comfort, I am not going upstairs or to the basement. Good-bye is finished here, where I stand. As I walk back through the foyer to the front door, I place my hand on the door knob and feel its smooth, cool brass surface. I open the door, step out and hear the click of the lock as the other door closes behind me. I don't look back. I feel a lightness and anticipation for the new memories to be sculpted.

The car is packed, and our dog, Karma, is in the back seat with thoughts of her new kingdom racing through her white, Bischon head. Little does she know she will be sharing her once perfect empire with alligators. Guess where our new home is? The Sunshine State, Orange Capital of the World, and home to the World of Fantasy – built by a mouse.

During our nine hundred mile drive to our new home, we had a constant companion named Norman, tropical storm of the year. It followed us through Virginia and the Carolinas and on toward Georgia. This storm pelted the northeast and the southern states with torrential rain and sixty mile an hour winds. The first day, we took turns driving. Sometimes it was easier to pull into a rest stop and wait for a little break in the weather. The scenic drive we had hoped for was now a postcard memory.

After hours of driving, we tried to find a place for lunch, which really turned into dinner, but we both ordered breakfast. After enjoying our scrambled eggs, toast and sweet tea – welcome to the south – we paid the bill and set out to find a hotel for the night. But every one we stopped at had no vacancy. I felt like Mary riding into Bethlehem: no room at the inn. Motel Six didn't even leave the light on for us. Pulling off the Interstate, we finally did find a hotel with the vacancy sign flashing. Three cars dotted the parking lot. We pulled on our rain gear and made a dash for the entrance. The Altered State Motel charged twenty-one dollars a night for a double – roaches were extra. I didn't care.

"Oh, Michael, we can't drive any longer, we need to sleep! Let's just take the room! You grab the Lysol – I have the suitcase."

We ran against the rain and when we unlocked the door, we recalled vivid images of the Bates Motel. The lights were dim – what a blessing – the bed damp and musty, and the four pillows on the bed shared twelve feathers. We sprayed the room, put towels on the floor to walk to the bathroom, and finally decided to sleep in our clothes. We put the hoods of our raincoats on our heads so we didn't have to put our faces near the pillows.

"Oh, Michael, this is romantic, almost like our first camping trip, but this time I can see the stars through the hole in the ceiling. Life is so full . . .oh, Michael, come close to me, look at the stars. What a night to remember, at least the storm has calmed."

As I started to fall asleep next to Michael, I thought of our first days together, but it was the nights that made me love this handsome man even more. Tonight was the pinnacle of our marriage: lying face-to-face with the large teeth of our zippers rubbing against each other, the touch of Michael's hand around the hood of my raincoat. I could sense my blood rushing and my heart racing. I thought, *"Oh, how old am I? Maybe I am just a slut in a raincoat heading to Florida for a new beginning. Do I need a new life? My old one was exciting – filled with children, laughter, and memories. Do I need a new home? My old one was comfortable, filled with furniture, magazines, and photos.* Some questions have no answers and some questions have only the answers you really don't want to hear.

"Oh, Michael, get up. The sun is out." He looked at me and his face still showed the lines from his plastic PJ's, but at least he wasn't wet. It took us ten minutes to get out of the motel, into the car and on the road to try to find a place for breakfast.

"Oh, Michael, I am so hungry."

"Tina, what we really need is a shower. We smell like plastic trash bags and it's starting to get hot."

"We can take off the raincoats and pull out clean shirts from the trunk."

"I need a shower," Michael shouted.

Then on the top of a hill just ahead was a huge billboard for gas, food and showers. My husband veered into the parking lot and hurried me out of the car. I realized we were surrounded by huge semis. I said, "Good Christ, Michael, it's a truck stop! I will absolutely not take off my clothes to shower in this place."

"Geez, we stink, Tina."

I stamped my foot and insisted, "I will not shower here!"

My husband knew when my mind was made up. He shook his head and said, "Tina, just get back in the car."

As we pulled out and headed south on I-95, the air was soft and warm. Our hopes for our new life behind the gates were soaring.

When we pull up to the front gate of the community, the security guard checks for our names, welcomes us, and offers directions to our village.

"Oh, Michael, now we are *Village People*."

"Shut up, Tina."

We are so excited we have forgotten we didn't have any lunch.

"Oh, Michael, let's eat at the clubhouse. We can get the flavor of the community and get a look at the pool and gym."

Michael was tired, but as usual, he did everything I asked. "Happy wife, happy life," was his motto and it served him well.

The dining room at the clubhouse was busy but we found a table overlooking the pool and the fountain. Our waitress, Janet, brought the menus and told us the specials for the day. I was captivated by her long blond hair, long pink fingernails and very long eyelashes. She was just long. *Is this the look of the other women in our community?*

We were so excited to see our new house and shared with Janet that we were new homeowners. "Nice," was her reply.

After Janet, the bundle of enthusiasm, walked away, we looked at each other and laughed. *Maybe we do smell.*

"Oh, Michael, hurry and eat, so we can go see the house."

"Let's hope the water has been turned on," Michael cried.

When we drove up to the new house, the moving van was waiting in the driveway for us. I could feel the tears starting to fill my eyes and my throat was burning. *Why did I feel this way?* My thoughts started to change like the wind, fast and furious, soft and calm, blowing and colliding. *Could two lives fit in a twenty foot moving van? Shouldn't there be more?*

I looked at the front of our home and had the strangest vision. *What if the house is built like a doll house with no back walls? We would be able to move from room to room like actors in a play, but have to keep away from the edge: no shouting or fighting in full view for all to see.* These unusual thoughts took flight as quickly as they began, but this feeling of transparency stayed with me. To us, this four bedroom, three bath home was our Florida Palace. We chose neutral colors, hardwood floors and an upgraded kitchen, complete with a convection oven, whatever that does. The most outstanding feature was the view of the pond. The sun danced and sent ripples of rainbows across the pond.

This is the feeling we hoped for, peace and dreams for our future together. We were brought back to reality when the movers started to surround us with boxes and furniture. We forged a path to the lanai for one more look at our estate when our neighbors called to us.

"Welcome! Moving day is a bitch," they shouted, walking toward us with drinks in their hands and huge sparkling smiles on their faces. "Welcome to Sunrise Village, I'm Bo Deebe and this is my wife, Cappy."

"It's a pleasure to meet you both," we said, and in turn, introduced ourselves.

Bo invited us to join them on their lanai and enjoy the tropical drinks Cappy had made. Their lanai was a paradise filled with parrot pictures, parrot planters, parrot placements and as the crowning glory, green as pond slime, sat Jerry, the parrot, king of the house.

"Tina, darling, come sit."

I moved the parrot pillow and sat at the high glass top table while Bo motioned for Michael to sit or as he suggested, "Take a load off."

"Cappy, what the hell is that smell? Smells like mildew. Did you clean Jerry's cage?"

"Bo, darling, I cleaned it yesterday. Remember I used the Wall Street Journal to line the bottom of the cage like you told me? You said it was the only thing *that* paper was good for. Let's just have our drinks and snacks, forget about the smell, I'll just turn the fans on."

I couldn't even look at Michael because I knew where the smell was coming from, but I was happy to let the blame fall on Jerry. I guess it's because I hate birds and if he belonged to me, God forbid, I would open the window and let that damn parrot fly away. I asked Bo if the parrot knew any words and with great enthusiasm and pride Bo told us Jerry's favorite line was "Jerry rules." This little green beast sat on one foot and repeated "Jerry rules" three times before Bo told him to knock it off, to which Jerry replied, "Mean Bo." We continued our conversation like a meet-and-greet session, exchanging names of our home towns, details of our family – three children, one dog, and a Florida dream house.

Bo asked, "Do you play golf?"

Michael's eyes started to glisten as he spoke in his golf voice, "I am *fore* all things golf, do I love golf, hell yes."

"Well, I will make sure you can play in our preferred tee-time group on Monday, Wednesday and Friday at 8:05. We are fierce, Mikey, play for money, and never tolerate cheating unless you use creative math – some of the boys just can't count. Their score of 90 turns into 85 depending on how many beers they drink. You will get used to it, Mikey."

The days after we move in marbled together like colors that complimented each other, and make the others appear brighter and more vibrant. We meet new neighbors, play golf, and learn the latest gossip over drinks at the clubhouse. This life was proving to be far removed from the style Michael and I led before we became Village People. Our new friends are older and more experienced. Two and three marriages are common, if the couples we met were married at all.

Snowbirds became the word of the day. *It reminds me of my bird hate.* We discover that someone was murdered in the house next to us, maybe a reason it was vacant for two years. They never found the killer but a person of interest still lives in the community. We thought that the roving guard would help to deter crime but it's hard to catch a murderer when you drive around the community in a golf cart.

Dinner each week at the clubhouse is an exciting night. Trivia keeps the memory sharp and water aerobics keeps your butt from sagging to the ground. Michael is elected to the Board of Directors and is responsible for the smooth operation of the restaurant. The last person who held this position retired and moved to a psychiatric facility. The only thing Michael knows about a restaurant is how to make reservations, but he is learning the complex operation of a Homeowners Association and how to navigate the choppy waters of men in power. The HOA is involved in a lawsuit concerning owners who park their car extended over the sidewalk, plant flowers near the golf course, and add a tree to the proposed landscape design without permission. The new owners next to us paint their home Sunset Beige also described as Tangerine. This encourages violation sanctions from the Board to the Tangerine lovers. They are banned from the clubhouse for three months and their lawsuit is scheduled. Last week, two couples were escorted from the restaurant after a shouting match over who had the largest piece of prime rib.

Sitting on the veranda at the clubhouse, we look over the pond at the sunset. "Oh, Michael, why can't it be peaceful like this all the time?"

"People are just insane when it comes to their perceived entitlements, Tina. When I think back to our first few months, we were learning the protocol of a HOA, who to be nice to, who to kiss ass when you needed something, and who you could boss around because you were on a committee."

Bo and Cappy are still Village People, the house next to us is still Tangerine, and the few in power still rule the community. Our time in Florida is drawing to a close. Michael has been diagnosed with lung cancer and needs to have surgery. *Life in Paradise, what does it mean? It can't be only rules, violations, and people fighting over nonsense.*

We are packing once again and have sold our house to an excited couple from the Midwest. Hopefully, the new owners have not made the same decisions about where and how to live based on palm trees and blue skies.

We will make the trip back home to Pennsylvania one last time. As we pull out of the driveway, we notice a large object flying close to our car. I can't believe the image – there was Jerry. Someone got smart and opened the door to his cage. As I watch him rise and fall, his beautiful wings keep in rhythm with the breeze. My senses flow together and our new journey is as necessary as breathing.

We all need to spread our wings and fly, soar and sail among the clouds, and connect with our soul call. We have learned to listen for the echo of our hearts and follow its tune. We may never realize where our call will take us. But we are content. Our soul is in charge.

THE WINE BOTTLE

by

Lore Pearson

When I was a kid I heard that you could put a message in a bottle and maybe someone across the sea would get it and save you. I never believed. That's until I was in a midlife funk. Actually the whole adventure of tossing wine bottles to sea redefined what I thought about life and love.

I guess the best place to begin is to give a little emotional history.

* * * * *

I hadn't drunk alcohol, even wine, for a long time. My abstinence evolved from the Seventies riot at Kent State University where I had learned a sufficient lesson about myself, our culture, and demonstrating against the National Guard. The experience with me against them was traumatic.

In retrospect I realized my passion for political science drove me to drink because of a common frustration lawyers share. We generally don't see justice served. Being an American idealist, this drove me nuts. I wasn't a temperate person, so a night with the demons always meant too many drinks. Though innately I knew that there was no way I could pursue a constitutional law practice without becoming a drunk or going dry. I communed with that ol' devil-may-care.

Years of tribulation exemplified that I had chosen the wrong career. Pessimism ate at me. Stressed-out was the current diagnosis with a deluge of drugs prescribed. For me it translated simpler: I had to get away from my law practice or go crazy.

A prescribed dosage laced with alcohol resulted in a near death experience where, from outside my body, I watched a doctor desperately use a defibrillator on my heart with no success. They pronounced me dead. A nurse leaving the ER noticed my finger twitch.

"Lucky girl," the doc with pursed lips scolded. His drawn face frowned as I awoke still smelling smoke from my bra-burning motherland, convinced I had to make sense of my life.

This experience triggered an emotional uprising within me to take a moral stand. Working in a private agency advocating the rights of battered women and children was just the right chemistry, for my father had been terribly abusive to mom and me. Not surprising then that in my primary years I had hoped to make a difference for women in society. Now I was ready. I changed professions into a low-level financial lifestyle, working for something I truly cared about.

During this humble soul-searching time, I decided to stay away from drugs, including prescribed antidepressants. The challenge to seize the day took tremendous inner struggle at first. Eventually I found peace enough to marry and start a family. For a couple decades, I was really happy.

Then the acrimony of my husband's fear of age and death crept in resembling a slithering snake in the grass with friggin dissolution papers in his mouth. Divorce? More like loss. Loss of worth, happiness, and stability, of companionship and love. The love that I trusted would be forever.

A series of further depressing events materialized within two years of my divorce: The agency for abused women and children closed; my adult child had historical anger; my dying mother was fiercely afraid of hell, and she was not appreciating me changing her diapers. My unreasonable financial concerns were endlessly boring. And the eye-of-my-soul was sore from searching for that ideal soul mate who I believed would solve all of the above angst, somehow.

"Wine! A little liquor's good for your heart," mother's doctor urged. "It'll help de-stress and relax you, dear. Remember what

Ogden Nash said, 'Candy is dandy, but liquor is quicker.'"

"Ogden who?" I asked myself, knowing very well that old doctor dearest had pushed a button even though I'm thinking, "How can dulling your mind get anything to work better." But not to question the wisdom of those who have taken the Hippocratic Oath. My darling ex was an international corporate physician of great merit. Problem was that he got into examining more than sick bodies.

Mom's doctor didn't realize I'm an indulgenist and a health fanatic. Basically, I believe if something's good to consume, it's good for you morning, noon, and night. Hard liquor made me feel dull, which feeling made me mad. That was not for me! Now wine, well, it gave a tingly warm feeling in a religious way. Jesus' first miracle was turning water into wine at a wedding giving blessed inspiration. Thus the tradition of feeling unduly satisfied while drinking wine.

My family thought I was drinking too much. They encouraged: "Get a life!"

"Stop feeling sorry for yourself!"

"We all have it hard, by God!"

This love affair with wine was about me. I felt compromised when more wine bottles wound up in my trash than water bottles. But who was watching? My family was involved in their respective niches. I was on my own recognizance. I probably said this before, but really, I was okay with that. In all honesty, I didn't want to hear: *By not being moderate for godsake, you're hurting yourself,* from people who were doing a decent job of doing just that, hurting me for years.

The messages

The first message said, "Help me, somebody," ending with sig and contact info. I corked it in the day's fav wine bottle and stalked down the outside hallway, letting it spelunk in the garbage chute.

* * * * *

Guess I had better rewind a bit and mention that I had been grand fathered into a condo owned by my older boyfriend, of course, in great shape. Harrison tagged me the only g-string touting resident on the second floor of his Flori-dah senior's complex, thinking that was so funny. At first I laughed, too.

The sex was good with Harrison but awakening from the horrendous pain of bonding with his irresponsible libido wasn't really worth it. He didn't intend to commit. Nor tell the truth. So I needed to get away from him before hate overcame me. But how? So I read how-to books; some were a temporary fix. Others made me angrier. "Why can't I love myself enough to leave this womanizer?" I pleaded with me, myself, and I. But the girl wasn't listening. By the time I disrobed for bed, I forgot my needs.

Then the oddest thing happened. Harrison had a fatal heart

attack while we were having sex. It was awful squirming out from under his limp body and calling 911. I felt so guilty, like a criminal.

I mourned for weeks. The tears dried in a moment of truth; I had to admit that it was good to get free of this liar-liar-cats-on-fire. "But what now?" I asked. Only thing I saw was that I was in a mental state like Norah Jones' song: I was soaking my soul with wine . . . galore.

The messages continue

The idea of secret messages in wine bottles continued to give me a lift that something magical could happen for me once again, no matter my age.

But I wanted to hide my lost soul. So I'd wait until late, until the hearing aids of my neighbors were off so they wouldn't detect the sound of the bottle hitting the bottom of the metal trash canister.

One day while I was checking Facebook I felt particularly odd. I swore I heard neighbors gab as they shuffled past my dining room picture window. "Do you think she's a drunk?"

"She should just leave now that Harrison's dead."

Was I paranoid? It was reasonable to guess these folks had no perplexing thoughts outside their fragile bodies except how their friggin condo association comported itself this month. For if my life was even a smidgen interesting to them, they would have figured

194

that health conscious "she" would have been dumping Arizona green tea bottles down the ol' chute.

To the seashore

Silly girl. My harvest of soulful messages was not getting to the sea, of course. They were being crushed at some landfill with the rest of the scraps of my life from some yesteryear. Like the diamond ring inscribed, "until death do us part," securely wrapped in a tissue (because a stone was loose) and laid on the night stand. So instead of taking it for jewelry repair as asked, my turn-a-deaf-ear husband mistaking it for a snot rag, threw it in the trash. It was buried with locks from our kids first haircut which locks their daddy insisted be tossed during our hundredth move, supporting his career changes which was to make our lives so very wonderful in the long run. But where was he when I became the fool of his lies? Bali? Hawaii? Like the zombie I had been recycled into from divorce, all such precious matter - rings and locks, etc. - was gassed by tons of toxic crap upsetting the environment.

The concept of another dear thing of mine putrefying in the bowels of the earth grew unbearable. I needed to do this thing the right way and go to the sea.

Ceremoniously one sleepless Sunday I drove to Clearwater Beach, swam out as far as I could in the crystalness of the Gulf of Mexico, and cast my first bottle to sea before sunrise.

Superstition itched at me to cast away each bottle religiously in succession. No wetting the angst of my brain until I'd jettisoned the vessel from yester evening. Flying fear? Whatever the analysis, I had to do it just that way.

I didn't have time to daily go to the Gulf. So I cut back drinking to accommodate my ubiquitous passion to systematically fling messages for help, to the precincts of the turquoise-mind-of-the-deep; that turquoise emblazoned in a child's heart from the first day she was allured by the sea.

The boat ride

My passion was no longer satisfied with trips to the beach. Hitching a ride on a local gambling boat for sixty bucks a shot worked emotionally for me. Bon voyage.

I didn't make friends right off, hoping no one was looking as I arrived on deck, opened my oversized Fendi bag, and pitched my messenger, my holy grail, overboard.

Each time was transforming. I'd stand there struck by the significance of the moment I had created. I was casting a piece of my heart with the profound conviction there was someone magical looking for me. Maybe not to-the-letter, but the idea was clear. His body energy and spirit of mind would be well matched with mine. My message would provoke him to find me. I knew it sufficiently to pledge I would never give up. My body would die in the lonely confines of my dream before I would ever stop hoping for the right man. A man who didn't want to rob me emotionally blind or drain my bank accounts, who could fend-off cranky relatives without accusing me (consciously or unconsciously) of being worse than they were. A man who would make love, not F-my-brains-out as if that was desirable, and one who would deliver my soul with the gentle touch of an angel. In a word: a virtuous man of means. And we looked good together. Talk great talk. Walk that walk. A creative waldorf who's lots of fun.

There I stood that virgin night enveloped in a lover's ritual gazing into the mysterious depths, wet from the sea breeze by the time someone discovered me. "Oh, my dear. You are soaked," some old lady said.

I kept staring at the sea. She left after patting me on the back.

As time passed I was friendlier when awakened in the midst of my-dream-is-desperately-better-than-my-life.

The first cruise

My lust to get my thoughts deeper to sea became insatiable. The first cruise was within my budget.

I got a fantastic price to the Bahamas in the fall. I learned, as someone who has done their homework knows, it is still hurricane season there in - October - the reason for the cut-rate cruise. Mahogany. My eyes looked mahogany maroon when I returned home.

With anticipation my journal recorded getting, ". . . time and time again, grails off to the diamond sea of love. I feel fortunate to have given part of my living soul to the Atlantic. I await the joy of love which as yet is out of my compass range."

Expensive cruises

I cashed CDs; then dipped into 401K plans, to afford luxury liners.

I hatched some peculiar thoughts on my cruise around Indonesia. It must have been the ghosts of corporate patriots cheating on their wives which I felt in my bones. Maybe it was Bali. Whatever! I envisioned that just maybe if I signed a message with a drop of my blood, my last drop of hope, somehow some Cosmic-Giver-of-All-Good would understand how serious I was and would see how much of me is being drained away waiting for true love. (I mean, my friends had true love.) Then I thought of a shark choking to death on my bottle, drawn to it by the smell of *my* blood. Actually, that sounded like a good idea. Sharks scared me like husbands. But then again, I wasn't into body piercing for blood.

"Pitiful." I moaned, stirring in my cabin bed the next morning thinking of the almost blood-letting event of last night.

"Ouch!" I cried after accidentally whacking my head on the wine bottle left in my bed when I crashed in the wee hours. (I recalled nursing it like a baby.)

Last cruise

The last cruise proved to be the Omega of the Alpha. A painful yet salutary lesson reacquainting me with my reason for being: to love and to be loved.

I felt a need after another luxurious cruise to dignify my

bottle jousting, noting in my journal, "The psychology of my obsession may help others. The pattern seems obvious. I talk about the first this, the first that. True. Each toss is like the first because it brings me closer to the desired climax. Well, all but the last."

OMG! I didn't know what the hell I was talking about when I read my journal entry in the morning. Yet, no matter. I was not about to stop drinking wine again.

That evening, my brain spongy from lots of wine, about midnight on the other side of my normal world, outside *Puerto Palma de Mallorca, Espana*, the largest of the Balearic Islands, my sheets stained burgundy, I'm pondering: "Is that blood or wine?" . . . I was grumbling as my drunkenness took on a life of its own. Next I knocked the wine bottle off the side table in my cabin-nest-a-hide-a-life. My whole world was so fuzzy all I could do was hope that I wouldn't have remorse.

Not wanting to be found out upon going ashore in the morning, I removed the stained sheet from my bed and discretely, creeping up on the promenade deck, tossed it into the forgiving sea. I peered at the sheet religiously in the light of a full moon; it was moving across the water's surface. The sea playing with my naked sheet, floating it, soaking it to death in a ballet, pirouetting it into the blue depths of an abyss which my childhood had dreamt was God.

I wondered, *What if I had aborted myself into the azure Mediterranean Sea – the silk of my body like a film of death?* The proverbial selfish *you-devil-you* was haunting me.

Guilt set in. "I'm an environmental scum bag. I've suffocated innocent fish. What has my psyche come to?" my journaling wept before breakfast.

Magic on shore

There I was oblivious of yesterday's regret, popping a new cork, in love with Spain. Wondering: *How could a wine bottle possibly get me to this glorious Spanish island - the most enchanting place on earth? Life is paradoxical. I never expected to be enhanced in such a way. Ensalada de mango, my favorite for lunch. Dinner with the splendor of Mediterranean olives and garlic, garlic, garlic .*

And my journaling took poetic license. "I love coming home to Mallorca. Palma at the La Seu Cathedral set my soul on fire, and on its steps the gold-body-painted Mime hugged me. Harbor lights sparkling with humongous yachts. My true love probably on one, but Greek - - I don't think so. Vespas zooming. *Habla Espanol* with neighboring hotel guests nestled on their balconies in mosquitoless pleasure (unlike my Florida digs.) Then through the *tunel* to Port de Soller, from the lighthouse gasping at the crimson sun setting around 9:15 PM. I love time here. It is slow. It is fast. Its life-rhythms are not wound by clocks. Hearts flowing in the cosmos now, gently moving *novios y novias.* Joy in knowing Mallorca, that one is not alone here but rather embraces space with no offense to individual moments, ceremoniously dancing demons away in Fire Vespers. It was worth the incredible struggle it took to get here. That I am here is God. (Note: Look-up ritual.)"

Calla (cove at) Deia, Mallorca

The children played at the water's edge with even their grandmother's breasts sunbathing. Moons of breasts bare to the world. *How can I be shy of the very thing I thrived by. Motherhood in all its manifestations is well. Life is sustained.* I did it for the first time. Flung that contraption off my breasts, unlocked my arms, and smiled.

A private yacht cruised into the port over calm waves. *Is he coming to me with my message?* I hoped.

Crew took the yacht's speed boat into the womb of the cove to check out the surroundings for more than sharks. The area was obviously approved. For following next, against my wishes, were rich bitches in Onassis sunglasses, silhouetted by their barrel bellied gods. I sat in the narrow limits of Calla Deia like a tromped sand flea, envying more than I understood. I closed my eyes to dream my message. The wine bottle was my muse.

As my eyes blinked open in the sunlight, he was looking into my soul. Blinded by more than sunlight, I squinted. He greeted me in Catalan. I couldn't remember a word of Spanish. He smiled at me. His white teeth seemed bigger than his face and sparkled as he stared at my breasts. He didn't speak English. Our eyes met in a moment emblazoned in my mind. Something wonderful had happened. But what? As always that was the enormous question of the day. What is really going on here? Sex. Love. Both for a change? How could I know that this time was to be it? *He hasn't mentioned the message in the bottle yet,* I worried as he knelt beside me with Gladiator ripped light chocolate color abs.

Oh, sweet mystery it was a wondrous night. And I was not for a moment distracted by the storm. The next day's newspaper reported 1,500 lightning bolts. We had breakfast and then the bomb hit.

Basically, I refused him the money he asked for, speaking in English. I took a taxi back to the cruise ship, half crying, half battering myself, but the bitch in me argued back, "He should of asked for it up front. Would have saved us both the bother . . . . and screw this. There's no hope."

All aboard!

I checked my email. And there it was. A message from a man named George V., who had recovered a wine bottle with a message I had written in the winter. My hope was rekindled.

I replied, getting it returned, tagged undeliverable. Then the computer had a glitch. My reaction changed from immediacy to complacency to a sense that tomorrow will bring more news though I spent the whole night trying to figure out from where I had cast it.

Tomorrow was not an email day.

The plane took off with me journaling before landing on American soil. "Monday, August 9, 9:30 PM. Even the pounding feet of the woman with the Irish accent and her two teenagers in their respective single airline seats behind me and me with oodles of room with a three-seater row all of my own in front of them, and them continuously agitating whichever of the three seats I sat in (before the sprawl) couldn't make me take a negative slant. Actually, I laughed to myself at first that their foot gyrations were a subtle back massage which they may tire of quickly. Then I said it to her. 'Thank you for the back rub.' She burst out, 'YOU CAN'T HAVE ALL THOSE SEATS.' But yes I did have them. And I didn't regret it for a second, feeling special was my turn. Oh, to drive someone equally barmy on my return home, for that same reason – that the whole world is mad, and it's not my fault."

Last wine bottle

On Wednesday, I went to the beach near home. And there it was. I ran to it, resembling a kid's legging-it to a candy store. I knew there must be a message in it from him. Haphazardly, I broke it upon the nearest rock and unscrolled the scripture. "Oh, shit!" I blurted-out to my embarrassment as a Nun (looking more like a penguin than my off-color mood could stand) walked hand-in-hand with a school of children stringing along behind her like a knotted kite-tail.

It was so pitiful. It read: "Someone help me, please. imyours@tampabay.rr.com, Kate." I had found my message, not *his*.

Like I was recycled not only from divorce but in a bottle.

On the way home I stopped for lunch at Hungry Dick's. Then rushed in the condo and swallowed an overdose of ipecac, a relic from my teens. I vomited morsels of deep-fried cod, French-fries, pickles, and coleslaw. I recognized the bile taste in my throat. I had become acquainted with it long ago, an anorexic hopeful, trying to beat the battle-of-the-bulge and land Mr. Right by inducing vomiting after a gorge session with the devil, food.

By morning I knew it was over. Maybe not drinking wine, but the bottle fetish and peccadillo that any man could carry my baggage and fill my interior life with love.

In the afternoon I got another email from George V., which reversed my thinking 360. *God, he did find it. What was I thinking to cast my dreams to the wind yesterday? He's found me.* Upon his request I sent him personal info.

About 5:00 AM the next morning I get this irate phone call from some guy, who finally identified himself as George, and who swore he'd sue me if I ever threw another #@!!% bottle of any sort in the sea again. It almost blew his engine. (I couldn't fathom how the message wasn't shredded. What luck!)

"Okay, okay. I'm very sorry. But don't start threatening me. I'm an attorney. And anyway, Mr. Sourpuss, I've decided to stop wishing." Click.

He didn't have to shout at me. My childish fantasy was down the drain. And my adult realization was emerging: Love is not out there, anyway. Chemistry is out there. The message was to discover the love inside me.

ABOUT THE AUTHORS

DEANNA J. BENNETT is a compulsive writer who has published short technical, travel, management and general articles and has a murder mystery and a fact-based fictional immigrant story in final edit. She loves hanging with writers and aspiring writers, traveling , and husband Tom, her partner in their acting company.

TRISH COMMONS writes in the Tampa Bay area where she lives with her husband and two golden retrievers. She graduated from St. Petersburg High School and University of South Florida and taught English in Florida public schools. Her work in progress is a young adult historical novel. Her passions are grandmothering, research and volunteering.

ARLENE TRAINOR CORBY began writing when she and her newly retired husband traveled cross-country in a pop-up camper. The ELCL Writer's Workshop helped her put these adventures and lessons learned into her book, *Popping Up Across America, A Travelogue and How To Guide*. Never expecting to be an author, she has found joy in the written word and camaraderie of other writers.

ROBERT J. DOCKERY worked as a naval architect and later a mechanical engineer before entering Georgetown Law School. After practicing law in the New York area, he decided to simplify his life with a move to Florida. He currently writes and teaches fine art painting. Bob is married and has two daughters.

RUTH DUNCAN is a transplant to Florida from Southern California. She has published magazine articles, poetry and short stories. She is currently writing a novel set in the turbulent racial background of the 60s. Her spare time focuses on rescuing stray cats and kittens and finding them forever homes.

JOHN A. DUNN, an aspiring writer since 1999, joined the ELCL Writers Workshop to improve his craft. His current project is a historical fiction time travel novel, *Call Me Master*, set in America in the early 1800's. John is a Brown belt in karate, and volunteers his Fridays at First Presbyterian Church in Brooksville, FL.

MAUREEN LACEY is a Philadelphia native and a graduate of Immaculata College, transplanted to Florida where she is a staff member at East Lake Community Library. She is an artist and writer. Her two completed works are a biography of her late actor son, and a novel with both worldly and other-worldly characters.

MARGE MARANTE, a registered nurse and avid equine enthusiast, lives with her husband in Palm Harbor, Florida, where she is at work on a paranormal medical thriller.

LORE PEARSON is a freelance and short story writer, an award-winning poet currently working on a blog, *A Year of Inside Out*, a heartfelt daily posting about her wilderness experience. She does TV commercials and lives in the Florida wetlands area with her horse, Masquaw, and two goats, Ruthie and Mary-Carole.

DOROTHY ANN SEARING published an award-winning essay at age twelve and has been writing everything from technical product literature, to corporate training courses, to safety newsletters, ever since. She won an honorable mention in a Writers Digest short story contest and is working on her first novel, a bodice busting tale of greed, rape and murder about desperate people in desperate situations.

PAT STEFURAK hails from Brielle, New Jersey and thrives on writing about days gone by. She is currently focused on a novel depicting life as an American teenager living in Mexico City during the 1950's. She lives in Florida with her outrageous Sheltie, Murphy.

Contact East Lake Writers Workshop or the individual writers at

floridamind@gmail.com